Cat-atonic

by

Sue C. Dugan

The Cat with Nine Lives, Book 2

Cat-atonic

Cover Art by *The Wild Rose Press, Inc.*

The Wild Rose Press, Inc.
PO Box 708
Adams Basin, NY 14410-0708
Visit us at www.thewildrosepress.com

Publishing History
First Edition, 2023
Trade Paperback ISBN 978-1-5092-5281-7
Digital ISBN 978-1-5092-5282-4

The Cat with Nine Lives, Book 2
Published in the United States of America

Nick turned in his bed when his phone buzzed, and he glanced at the ID. Finally, a message from Cat! The text was wavy and didn't stay put. He wiped at his face, trying to clear away the fog. Those painkillers played tricks with his eyes, making the words move and rearrange themselves.

He squinted at her text:

—Help me! Please!—

Cat's words were bold and chilling. He reread it to make sure because sometimes his thoughts were those of someone else.

Nick swallowed the lump in his throat and immediately wrote back:

—What's wrong?—

He had to type the message several times to get it right. His fingers were numb and clumsy from inactivity and medication. He shifted on the bed but still couldn't get comfortable. The sheet felt like a tourniquet around his chest, pressing on his surgery site and making him gasp for air.

He held his breath—no return response.

Praise

Dedication

Cat-atonic is dedicated to my family for their love and support during the writing, editing, and publishing process. This book is also dedicated to my dear friend, Marti Tote, and her husband, Bob. They have weathered storms in their marriage that only strengthen their love and respect for each other. I must also thank Marti for her marketing expertise.

There are so many people to thank during and after the publishing process. The finished book is only the tip of the iceberg. These are the unsung heroes in making this book what it is today. First, I must thank Amy Tipton (Feral Girl Books) for her honest editing and suggestions that have strengthened my stories. Then I must thank all the wonderful people at The Wild Rose Press for their hard work behind the scenes, especially Dianne Rich. Dianne's attention to detail and willingness to format and edit my work has only improved it. I need to thank Barbara for reading *Cat-atonic* before it was published and giving me her honest feedback. I also want to thank my Tuesday afternoon critique group for listening and providing feedback on my work! You guys are the best!

And I must thank my friends who I have bored with story ideas, details, and plot twists. Thank you for listening with grace and good humor! And thank you for continuing our friendship!

Chapter 1

"Let me help you," Nick's mother said. She stepped into his bedroom and pushed a pile of shoes and socks aside, wrinkling her nose at their smell. "Phew! Nick!" She waved her hand under her nose.

When he didn't respond, she said, "We need to be at Dr. Garson's office in two hours." She sat on his bed and reached out her hand to his.

Nick shrugged away from her and painstakingly moved his body to sit and pushed his legs over the side of the bed, panting with exertion—his forehead itched with sweat.

"Shall I get the shower started?" she asked.

He shook his head. "No. No shower."

His mother frowned and wrinkled her nose again. "You need a shower, son."

Well, he didn't want a shower. Dr. Garson would get him like this or not at all. "No, it'll hurt my chest."

"At least let me help you dress."

Again, he said, "No."

"I put a clean pair of sweats on the chair," she said, standing and stepping closer to the clothing.

Nick stared dully at the green and white sweatpants and shirt with the Laketon High Lancers logo on the front—a knight on a horse with a sword.

His mother shifted her feet before saying, "If you don't need my help, I'll be downstairs."

She left, but not before giving him a concentrated look of concern and closing his bedroom door behind her. Nick could tell that she was worried by her slow steps and sagging shoulders. His parents were concerned about their only child.

Nick surveyed his bedroom. The bedroom he had had since they moved in when he was small. The bookshelves held memories—favorite books, his plastic army soldiers, and pictures of their family. Front and center was his favorite picture of him with his grandpa, who told wonderful stories about fighting the Germans during the war.

Is that how Nick had gotten his wartime memories? His grandfather's stories? The visions and memories started the moment Cat enrolled in school and told him... He grimaced and clenched his jaw. They were once boyfriend and girlfriend seventy years ago.

He gritted his teeth, pushed himself upright, and dressed. Too tired to go to the dresser for clean underwear, he decided Dr. Garson would get him unshaven, unclean, and commando, but the doc had probably seen worse.

Nick and his mother drove through the gunmetal, cold morning to the cardiologist's office—a rectangular building of gray that blended with the frost-laden morning. Most people waiting to see the cardiologist were old, like Nick's grandmother. He felt self-conscious being the only sixteen-year-old in the room.

Yet, here he was, a young man in a sea of gray, bald heads, hearing aids, canes, and walkers. The magazines on the tables were about freedom RVing, Best Places for Retirement, etc. Nick could see no sports or football mags.

His mother squeezed his hand before picking up a magazine and flipping through the pages. Nick could tell by her rigid back she wasn't particularly interested in new recipes, toning exercises, or the best places to retire. Her only concern was for Nick. He couldn't imagine what his deformity and surgery had put his parents through.

Finally, it was his turn, and they followed the nurse into the hall lined with examination rooms. The pictures on the walls were brightly colored and showed scenes of waterfalls, flowers, and cattle grazing in lush green fields—not images of late fall in Michigan.

"Step on the scale," the nurse said, and Nick did.

She tapped her pencil on the chart. "You've lost fifteen pounds."

"He doesn't have much appetite since his surgery," his mother said, hovering near his shoulder with a frown.

"Common," the nurse said, writing something in the chart.

"Nick?" his mother asked.

How was he to respond? He remained quiet and shrugged.

In the examination room, the nurse told him to take off his shirt and sit on the table, where she took his blood pressure and instructed him to wait for Dr. Garson.

The room was cold, and Nick shivered, feeling the goose bumps and raised hairs on his arms. He looked down at the incision in the center of his chest. It had faded from red to pink—a fat earthworm.

The cardiologist had a plastic replica of the heart on the counter. Nick got up, cinched in his sagging sweatpants, and picked up the model before sitting back down. The heart consisted of red, blue, and yellow colors denoting chambers and vessels.

His mother frowned when he got the model and gave him a slight nod.

"Good morning." Dr. Garson came in and shook their hands. "How are you feeling?" He listened to Nick's chest with his stethoscope.

Nick shrugged. He wasn't in the mood to talk, shower, or do anything else.

"He's been like this since we got home," Nick's mother answered for him, her fingers moving in a hopeless gesture.

"Like what?" Dr. Garson asked.

"Not talking, eating, or getting out of bed." She paused. "Right, Nick?"

He stared dully at them.

"Is she right?" Dr. Garson asked. He folded his arms and leaned against the counter, his full attention on Nick.

"Yes." He shrugged.

"Are you taking your meds?"

Which ones? He had yellow, green, and blue pills.

"Nick?" his mother asked.

"I guess."

Dr. Garson frowned. "You guess? You need to be taking all of them." Dr. Garson held up a hand. "Two are antibiotics, and one is an anti-depressant. Many people experience depression after surgery."

He was big-time depressed but had been that way before surgery.

The doctor took the model from Nick and tapped it while he talked. "I didn't get a chance to explain the operation because your surgery was an emergency." He inclined his head. "You had a fairly straightforward surgery to put a patch over the hole in your heart between the two sides, see?"

Nick looked where the doctor's finger rested. "There can be complications." The doctor continued. "Fluid retention, side effects from the anesthesia, infections. Those medicines are important to help you heal."

Nick's mother gave him a raised-brow look of questioning, concern, and reproach.

"I think a follow-up with a therapist would be good," Dr. Garson said, looking first at Nick and then his mother.

A therapist?

"Dr. Sara Beth Patar, one of the best pediatric psychologists in the area," Dr. Garson said.

They thought he was crazy. Catherine Anne Thomlinson, aka Cat, had messed with his head by telling him he was a reincarnated soldier. Was it a sin to be reincarnated? His father, a Methodist minister, thought so.

Chapter 2

Nick and his mother left Dr. Garson's and were pulling away when it started to rain. Not a gentle rain either—a continuous downpour, rain that obscured the windshield even with the wipers going at top speed.

"Wow," was all Nick could say.

"Wow, is right." His mother pulled over. "I can't drive in this."

They parked and listened to soft music on the radio.

"I guess we're stuck here," Nick said.

"Don't you love Michigan weather?" his mother mumbled and wiped at the condensation on the side window, but they only saw endless rain.

Nick wasn't particularly concerned. If he were at home, he would go to bed. This way, he could watch the waves of water run down and over their car, mesmerizing sheets of gray/blue. The intermingling of colors caused a stab of pain in his right temple. He gingerly rubbed the spot, wondering why rain would cause such a reaction in his head.

"Hmm." Nick reclined his seat and settled back. "I think I'll take a nap." A yawn escaped, slurring his words.

"Go ahead." His mother gave him an encouraging smile. "We might be here for a spell."

Nick settled back and was asleep, only to feel a tap

on his arm.

"You'll catch your death of cold," the cart driver said.

I covered my head with the remains of my Union blue coat as we waited out the storm. The rain didn't seem to deter the Rebels. Soaked or not, they continued pushing ahead. Hundreds of them, a continuous blur of blue/gray swarming over and around our hiding place.

Me and the cart driver stayed hidden in the trees, waiting and watching for the Confederate Rebs to pass. The rain, a deluge, made the cart's bed waterlogged and the bags of onions dark with moisture.

I tried sleeping, only to feel the cart move out of the trees.

"You still alive, Jonathan?" the cart driver asked. "We were stuck here for a right long spell."

"The Rebels gone?" Nick mumbled.

"What?" his mother asked.

"Nothing." He quickly sat up and scrubbed at his eyes. "Just a dream."

She put on her blinker, and they merged into the traffic, the wheels sending up waves of dirty water from the street. Nick felt disoriented and off balance as the unfamiliar scenery went by, all the while searching for the sea of gray amongst the cars and trucks. The Rebels were gone. Hallelujah.

Chapter 3

Nick turned in his bed when his phone buzzed, and he glanced at the ID. Finally, a message from Cat! The text was wavy and didn't stay put. He wiped at his face, trying to clear away the fog. Those painkillers played tricks with his eyes, making the words move and rearrange themselves.

He squinted at her text:

—*Help me! Please!*—

Cat's words were bold and chilling. He reread it to make sure because sometimes his thoughts were those of someone else.

Nick swallowed the lump in his throat and immediately wrote back:

—*What's wrong?*—

He had to type the message several times to get it right. His fingers were numb and clumsy from inactivity and medication. He shifted on the bed but still couldn't get comfortable. The sheet felt like a tourniquet around his chest, pressing on his surgery site and making him gasp for air.

He held his breath—no return response.

Nick tried contacting Cat again:

—*Tell me what's wrong. Are you hurt?*—

Cat's only real friends in Laketon were Veronica and Nick. Had she reached out to Veronica too?

Nick texted Veronica: —*Heard from Cap?*—

Veronica: —*Who?*—

Darn his clumsy fingers. He tried again: —*Cat*—

Veronica: —*No? How are you feeling?*—

Nick: —*Bitter.*—

Veronica: —*Sorry to hear that.*—

Nick: —*I mean better.*—

His fat fingers seemed to have their own mind—typing the wrong letters.

Veronica: —*Good. We miss you.*—

Nick: —*Do you know where she went?*—

Veronica: —*Oregon*—

Nick: —*Where in Oregon?*—

Veronica: —*Don't know.*—

He didn't know where either. Cat had been vague when she left. These messages didn't help with the gray swirl of depression he felt. Most of the smothering-wet-wool blanket feeling was his recovery from open heart surgery, but this message from Cat didn't help. He blew out his breath. How come she hadn't contacted him back? He lay back in bed and thought about the start of their junior year—a year he had high hopes for—wasn't as he had imagined it.

From the moment Cat whirled into the cafeteria like the dancer she was, things were never the same. His girlfriend, Emily, also reacted when Cat locked eyes with Nick. "Did you see the way she looked at you?"

Maybe she held his gaze for too long. He didn't know. "Like she knows you," Emily had said and explained girls had a sixth sense about "knowing" looks between guys and girls. Nick didn't know what that meant, although his mind began playing tricks on him, remembering places he had never been—although it seemed he had.

If that wasn't depressing enough, he felt like a failure as a son, boyfriend, athlete, and student. A heart defect had irrevocably changed his life.

If he could have rewound their junior year, he would have avoided Cat at all costs. But he couldn't have a "do-over" regarding her. So now he sat on his bed, his sheets a tangled, stale mess, recovering from open heart surgery with the message: —*Help me! Please!*— hanging over his head.

Chapter 4

Nick looked out the only window in his bedroom and watched the glittering frost on the branches. Outside it was raining leaves as the wind shook the trees with unseen hands. Football was over, the Michigan scout had come and gone, and Nick had blown that too—his one chance to make a good impression.

His life now resembled the pending winter weather—freezing, stark, and windy. The warmth of summer and his love for Emily had somehow turned cold when Cat enrolled in school and accused him of leaving her to die. Not die in his current lifetime, no, seventy years ago. She had somehow convinced him he was reincarnated from a WWII student soldier. And worse still, he began to believe he had been the soldier Jean Claude and had mistakenly tackled one of his teammates, thinking he was a Nazi soldier.

He rolled his eyes toward the sky, not seeing the gray, gunmetal clouds huddled on the horizon. Tackling your teammate was tantamount to kissing your reputation at school goodbye! A concussion diagnosis saved him from being labeled as a failure at football.

The skeletal branches of the maple tree outside Nick's window seemed to point an accusing finger in his direction, mocking him with *You're a crazy person, Nick Dupont!* Dr. Garson wanted him to see a shrink.

The craziness started with Cat's arrival and departure from Laketon High School.

He had tried forgetting about Cat until she sent him a chilling message:

—Help me! Please!—

Nick wasn't the type of guy who would ignore such a thing. He tried to follow his Christian upbringing. But he didn't know what to do since he wasn't sure where she was in Oregon, and she wasn't answering his text messages.

Then there was a knock on his bedroom door, shaking his thoughts away from his bleak outlook. "Are you hungry?" his mother asked, peeking around the door before stepping into the room.

His stomach was hollow, and he craved food, but nothing sounded appetizing. "Bread and water?"

She gave him a concentrated stare. "Interesting request." She folded her arms. "How about I fix you a couple of slices of toast?"

He made a face.

"Is that 'no' on the toast?"

"Toast sounds good," Nick said.

She picked up the dirty dishes on his desk before leaving him to stare out the window again.

What kind of future did he see for himself? Emily had broken up with him. Reasonable, sensible Emily was gone, and he had no one. Nick faced a long narrow black tunnel, much like the one he had experienced with Dr. Sims, except there was no bright light at the end. Cat had found Dr. Sims in Grand Rapids, and the doctor was supposed to help him remember when he had been Jean Claude. Was Nick remembering or just making stuff up? Or did he have a personality disorder?

Reincarnated was better than crazy.

He blew out his breath. He'd try Cat again.

—*Hey! Let me know U R OK.*—

Nick waited and then blinked at the knock on his door.

"Your toast," his mother said as she set a plate on the side table and sat on the edge of the bed. She frowned at the phone in his hand.

Nick thrust the phone into his pocket.

"Here!" She handed him the toast.

"Thanks."

"What are you doing?" she asked.

"Thinking about this school year." He slumped down into his desk chair.

She nodded for him to continue.

He shrugged. "Everything. Cat. Emily. My heart defect. Football"—he waved around his arms—"everything."

"Your heart defect was a surprise to us, too," his mother said, folding her arms and leaning against his bed. Her eyes changed and were laser focused on him. He recognized her social worker face. "Some heavy stuff in your life."

That was an understatement! He could see the headlines in the school newspaper: *Class leader and football standout Nick Dupont sidelined by Catherine Anne Thomlinson and Nazi soldier Bryan Cranden. Will he play football again? Or not?*

His mother eased toward the door. "I've got an online meeting in a few. Need anything else?" She waved her hand over the toast.

"I'm good."

She left, and he snuck another look at his phone,

but there was no response from Cat. Or anyone else, for that matter. He sat on the bed and began eating the toast until he felt a soft bounce on the bed as Minnie, his cat, jumped to his side and nestled herself against him. Nick stroked her head and felt her motor purr.

"There, there, Min…" Somehow, he wanted to call Minnie Stormy. But why?

He closed his eyes and envisioned a wet gray kitten hiding by an army tent. A cat called Stormy and a tent with a cross on the side—a medical facility on a battlefield. A primitive place where men moaned and cried out as they were operated on without anesthesia or modern tools.

He opened his eyes and studied Minnie's tortoiseshell-colored fur, so different from the cat he saw in his head. Minnie licked her paws and began cleaning her whiskers. There was something about that wet, starving cat that bothered him.

Then Stormy spoke to him in a voice inside his head.

"*You are always mine,*" she meowed. The fact she had spoken or even what she said didn't particularly surprise Nick. But why was he thinking of talking cats? He was crazy for real! Dr. Garson wanted him to see a psychologist. He could imagine their conversation about his mental state.

"I talk with cats."

"Interesting. Tell me more."

Would they put him in a straitjacket and take him away? It would be a fitting ending to the crazy year he had had so far.

Chapter 5

Nick texted Cat again:

—*Crazy. They want me 2 see a shrink now.*—

What would Cat think about that?

He had no time to consider her reaction when the doorbell chimed. He stowed his phone and turned on his side to hear who was at the door.

"I hope you don't mind me stopping by." A sweet-sounding voice floated up the steps and into his bedroom.

Nick rubbed his face. Emily?

"Of course not," his mother said. "We've missed you."

Then Emily said something Nick couldn't quite hear. Probably about their breakup and Cat.

"I brought him a card with his schoolwork."

"That's so thoughtful of you! Would you like to see him?" Nick's mother asked.

Nick shook his head. No, he didn't want to see her. He did, but not while he was all pathetic and sick.

"Only for a few minutes," Emily said.

"Nick!" his mother called.

"Yeah?" He covered his mouth. He shouldn't have answered, but it was too late.

"Emily brought you some things. Can she come up?"

He was quiet. His mother and Emily knew he was

awake. He shouldn't have answered, but now, if he didn't see her, Emily would think he didn't care about her, but he still did. "S…sure." He cared about both her and Cat.

Soon he heard, "Knock. Knock."

"Come in," he said, trying to sound sleepy and sore, which was true.

"Hi, Nick." Emily hesitated in the doorway. Her eyes surveyed the room, and then she wrinkled her nose.

"Sorry about the mess," Nick said. *And the smell.*

She gave a small giggle. "So this is what the locker room smells like!"

He motioned for her to come in, her pink-and-white-checked sneakers squeaking on the hardwood.

"Hi, yourself," he said—lame and weak sounding. But his heart beat faster at seeing Emily. Her glasses had slipped down on her nose, and she pushed them up—a too familiar gesture and one he loved—before giving him a tentative upturning of her lips.

And when he grinned back, she gave him her trademark smile that reached her eyes. That's why she had been his girlfriend and the junior class president. Everyone liked Emily with her genuine and friendly manner.

"I brought you homework and a card from our class." She set the pile on his desk.

"Thanks." He pushed the pillows behind him, so he was partially sitting up.

"I didn't know if you'd see me," she said, looking toward her shoes, moving them back and forth.

"Why not?" He sounded like an imbecile.

She tilted her head. "You know. The homecoming

dance. Our breakup. Cat."

"Cat's gone," he said.

"I know, but Veronica said you wanted to contact her."

With some difficulty, Nick found his cell phone and showed Emily the only message he had gotten from Cat since she left.

—*Help me! Please!*—

Emily stepped back with a frown as if his screen were on fire. "What does that mean?"

"I don't know. I sent Cat these messages, and she didn't get back to me."

He showed Emily all the messages he had sent, and her eyes narrowed in concentration. "She hasn't responded?"

"I don't know what to do." He put the phone back on the bedside table.

Emily sat on the edge of the bed, careful not to jostle him. "What can you do?"

"Dunno."

She took his hand. "I'm sorry."

"I don't know if she'll be back or not." He blew out his breath. "And I'm fine with that." That wasn't an entirely true statement. He cared for Cat too, but differently than Emily. It was hard to categorize his relationship with each girl.

Emily chewed her bottom lip, but they continued holding hands. "Do you mean that?"

"Yeah. Yeah, I do."

They sat looking at each other for what seemed an eternity, but it was probably five minutes. Emily untangled her hand from his and stood. "I better go." She moved her chin toward his desk. "Do you want me to open your card? Everyone in the junior class signed it."

Nick frowned. Had his least favorite person, Bryan, signed it too? Had Bryan written, "I'm on your side?" Nick rolled his eyes and shook his head at remembering tackling Bryan at the game, thinking he was a Nazi soldier. He'd never live that down.

"I guess you don't?" Emily asked, putting her hands on her hips.

"Sure, go ahead." He stifled a yawn.

"Why don't I come back, and we can go over the card when you're not tired?"

He nodded as his eyes shut, heard the door close softly, and fell asleep.

Nick dreamed in vivid colors when he took the antidepressant medicine. A tiny green pill made his sleeping thoughts alive in technicolor—the blood amplified ten times, suffocating him in the pulsating crimson goo.

He had dreams now about someone else—not Jean Claude but someone named Jonathan. Jonathan—an injured man from a different war than WWII. Jean Claude had died in the end, hadn't he? Dying trying to save the girl he loved—Chaton. Supposedly, Chaton was Cat in another life. He hadn't left Chaton to die on purpose, although Cat thought he had.

If Cat hadn't put the idea about being reincarnated in his head, would he even be having these thoughts?

Chapter 6

Nick's mother came in and set a tray by his bed. "I want you to try to eat something," she said, feeling his forehead.

"I'll try," he mumbled, moving away from her hand.

"You need to eat to heal from your surgery."

He turned away.

"You won't heal unless you give your body nourishment."

"I know." He blew out his breath but remained on his side away from her.

"Have you read the card Emily brought?" He rolled onto his back as his mother picked up the gigantic envelope.

"No."

"Would you like me to open it? It might be nice to read what your friends have written."

What friends? He hoped Gary was still his friend— they had been best friends forever. Nick had alienated almost everyone at school by his idiotic involvement with Cat, the girl with the strange notions. The girl had him doubting what he believed. She had planted the idea of Jean Claude in his mind. She had told him they were reincarnated lovers. She had somehow convinced him it was true.

"Sure."

"I'll read while you eat," she said and sat on the chair beside his bed.

Nick studied the grilled cheese sandwich, usually a favorite, but today the yellow cheese oozed like a pus-filled sore. A sore on...he racked his brain to remember where he had seen such a sore. Not on his body. No, someplace else. He swallowed slowly and painfully. The tomato soup gleamed like newly released blood.

"That doesn't look good, soldier," the surgeon said, wiping his hands on his blood-stained apron.

I shivered and sidled away, mumbling, "I'll be fine."

Nick picked up the sandwich, closed his eyes, and took a bite. It tasted better than it looked, and he realized how hungry he was. His stomach responded with a gurgle. He took another bite.

"Alrighty," his mother said, opening his card. She turned it so he could see the packed writing. "There are hundreds of names and well wishes for you, Nick," she said.

He blinked as if he didn't believe her and studied the card, recognizing some of the writing—like Emily's neat print. Emily had written a whole paragraph. What had she written? He imagined: *You're a dirty rotten dog who dumped me for that bitch, Cat.* Yet, she had passed around this card for him. He shrugged. She probably had to, as class president.

"Let's see..." his mother said, "Bryan wishes you a quick recovery."

Nick scowled. Bryan wouldn't wish that for his mother, much less for him. He grunted, and his mom arched an eyebrow.

"Coach Sullivan says he misses seeing you at

school and wants you back for football next year."

"Yeah, right." Nick rolled his eyes.

"Why do you say that?" his mother asked. "Dr. Garson said you could play again!"

The truth was, he didn't feel like playing football anymore. "We'll see," Nick said.

In the distance, he heard the downstairs telephone ring. "I better go," his mother said, leaving Nick alone. Only Minnie, the cat, remained and moved from the foot of the bed to his side.

He offered her a taste of his sandwich, to which she twitched her tail. "I know. That's how I feel too."

Minnie seemed to change and morph into another cat before his eyes. He blinked, but the gray cat from his dreams, Stormy, remained.

Was the cat connected with Jonathan?

He felt down his thigh, probing for the bullet. No bullet, but his leg was warm and hurt when he touched it. Oh, God, not again.

An absurd thought crossed his mind. "Are you Stormy?" Nick said to the cat.

Minnie twitched her tail as if contemplating his question. A voice in his head responded, *"You know who I am."*

Nick frowned as he patted and stroked the cat's head.

Soon he heard his mother's footsteps coming up the creaking stairs.

"Now, where were we?" his mother asked after returning from answering the telephone.

Nick was so shocked Minnie spoke to him in his head. He had lost track of why his mother was in his room.

"I can't remember."

"Don't you want to know who called?" his mother asked. When Nick didn't respond, she continued. "Dr. Garson was checking on you."

"What did you tell him?"

His mother paused. "I told him you didn't want to get out of bed still."

"And what did he say?"

"You need to move around to get your strength back."

"How can I do that if I'm dog tired?"

Dog tired? The cat voice in his head laughed.

"I bet you'd feel much better if you took a shower. Would you like me to help you to the bathroom?"

"No."

"We were hoping you'd join us tonight for dinner," his mother said.

"We'll see." If dinner was anything like lunch, he'd pass. "What are we having?"

"Roast. Grandma's coming for dinner."

He always liked seeing his grandmother.

"Maybe."

"Good." She patted his knee and then frowned at his sandwich with only a few bites from it. "You need to eat more than that."

Nick nodded, picked up the sandwich, closed his eyes so he wouldn't see the yellow pus cheese, and took another bite.

"See, that wasn't bad, was it?" his mother asked.

The cheese and bread stuck in his throat, and Nick thought he would be sick. He managed a nod.

"How about tomato soup?"

"I don't feel like soup today." He swallowed over

and over, trying to get the sandwich down his throat.

"I better get dinner started," his mother said before leaving.

When she was downstairs, he leaned over the side of the bed and vomited into the waste can that morphed into blood-soaked straw.

Chapter 7

When Nick's father returned from work, Nick heard his heavy tread on the creaky old farmhouse steps. Nick's father was a popular minister who visited sick parishioners and worked on his weekly sermons. It also helped he was a local hero of sorts. The Reverend Dupont played professional football with Detroit.

"How are you doing, son?" his father asked after coming into Nick's room and standing by his bedside.

"About the same." At times he felt like he was on an icy patch of road, his tires couldn't get traction, and he was spinning his wheels.

"Your mother says you're going to join us for dinner." His father looked over at the giant get-well card on the desk.

"Maybe. I want to take a shower first."

"I can help you with that." His father lifted his nose and sniffed.

"No, I'll be fine. Just help me out of bed."

Nick grasped the pillow to his chest to protect his incision, and his father helped push and pull him into a seated position at the side of the bed.

Nick was able to swing his wobbly, rubber-band legs to the floor. It was hard to believe just a few weeks ago, he was running down the field for a touchdown, and now he was as weak as a lamb.

"Easy does it," his father said as he helped Nick

stand. "Let me help you to the bathroom."

Nick opened his mouth to protest, but it felt good to lean on his father. They were alike in build, even though Nick still had some filling out to do—he was only sixteen, after all.

They walked slowly toward the bathroom. His father turned on the shower, put a towel within Nick's reach, and helped him off with his robe.

Nick stepped into the shower. The warm water rolled down his body.

"Do you want me to wait?" his father asked.

"I'll yell if I need you," Nick said, although he wasn't sure he could project his voice that far.

It felt good to be out of bed. Nick washed his face and body and let the water rain down, dipping his chin to check on his scar. Nick stayed under the shower until he felt the water temperature change. Hot to warm and then to cold. Shivering, he turned off the water and dried himself.

His father had left his robe on the corner of the sink. While Nick toweled off, he watched his face and upper torso come into view as the steam left the mirror.

His scar, partly covered by sparse hairs, was pinkish red and divided his chest evenly. Dr. Garson had said they cut through his breastbone to open his chest cavity during emergency surgery to repair the tiny hole in his heart. He was Humpty Dumpty, put together again.

He put on his robe and walked carefully back to his bedroom, putting one foot in front of the other and running his hand along the wall for balance and support. His father was sitting at the side of the bed reading the giant get-well card.

"Some nice sentiments in here," his father said, fanning the card.

"I only read a couple." Nick's heart raced at the exertion of taking a shower and walking down the hall, and he slumped down next to his father.

"You have a lot of friends at school," his father said.

Hardly. The students felt sorry. Emily must have guilted everyone into signing the card. He grimaced at the pity they must have felt for him.

He had alienated almost everyone this year except maybe Gary. Gary, his best friend since elementary school. Only Gary could overlook Nick's involvement with Cat.

"Shall I help you down the steps?" his father asked. "I need to pick up your grandmother for dinner."

"No, when you return. I think I'll take a nap while you're gone."

Nick smelled the aroma of roasting meat, and his stomach did a little gurgle. "Smells good," he said, much better than the cheese sandwich.

"I agree," his father said, squeezing Nick's hand before he left.

Nick lay back on the bed for a little cat nap. The thought sent an image of Cat across his brain. The last time he saw her while still in the hospital, she hadn't acted excited to be returning to Oregon. Or maybe it was when he told her he, as Jean Claude, had died trying to save her from the prison hole. The knowledge made him feel better about the whole reincarnation bit.

After Nick's nap and his father's return, Nick dressed and went downstairs for dinner. He leaned against his father and took the steps carefully and slowly, like his grandmother, who was waiting for him when he descended the stairs. She smiled when she saw him.

"Nick! Good to see you up and about!" she exclaimed. "You're walking better than your old granny here!"

Nick chuckled and kissed her on the cheek. "I don't think so, Grandma." Nick shook his head. "You could kick my tail in a race."

She grinned. "That's the old Nick I know!" She waved a hand over her walker. "Now, I have to use this contraption."

"Nothing wrong with that," Nick said, sitting in the chair opposite her. He had used a walker himself while in the hospital and when he first got home.

"I could ask you 'what's new,' though probably not much," she said.

"You'd be right, Grandma." He gave a one-shoulder shrug. "Doctor appointments."

She frowned. "I have plenty of those too. What kind of doctors?"

"A cardiologist."

"I've seen plenty of them for my ticker," Grandma said and sniffed at the air. "I sure wish your mother would hurry up. I'm starving."

Nick smiled. Come to think of it, he was too.

"When can you return to school?" she asked, always a former elementary teacher, wanting to know grades and what he was learning.

"Haven't even thought about going back," Nick admitted, "just concentrating on getting better."

Although getting out of bed and taking a shower had done wonders for his spirits. He felt much better, not one hundred percent—but the gray fog had lifted somewhat.

"Dinner," his mother called.

Nick eased out of the chair and pushed Grandma's walker toward her, and together they shuffled into the kitchen.

"Smells good, Mom," Nick said.

"I'm sure it's ten times better than at the Manor," Grandma said.

The Manor was a fancy name for the assisted living facility she resided in. If Grandma could have managed the stairs, she would have lived with them. Without a bedroom on the first floor, the option was out.

"I hardly think so," Nick's mother said, clearly pleased at the praise for her culinary talents.

"Beats hospital food any day," Nick said and was glad to see the worry lines on his mother's forehead lessen.

They sat, and Nick's father gave a blessing before carving the roast.

Nick squeezed his eyes closed as his father sawed at the meat, cutting pieces for everyone.

Nick thought he would be sick again. "I...I suddenly don't feel like eating." He pushed himself away from the table. His father's meat carving made him shiver.

His parents frowned. "But you love my pot roast!" his mom protested.

"Sorry." He patted his stomach. "Not tonight." *The sound of the saw cutting through flesh, tendons, and bone rasped at my stomach. And the metallic smell of blood. How could they stand the smell and sound?*

"How about some vegetables?" his father offered.

"Nick?"

Nick nodded and eased back down into the chair.

His mother served him potatoes, carrots, and a roll. "Gravy?"

He wanted nothing from the bloody stump of meat and said, "No, thanks."

Minnie came in silently and meowed loudly.

"You'll get fed, Stormy," Nick said, happy for the distraction.

"When did you change the cat's name?" Grandma asked, motioning with her fork toward Minnie.

"We didn't," his father said and dipped his chin toward Nick. "He's been a bit fuzzy since his surgery. The doctor says that's normal."

"I dreamed about a cat named Stormy," Nick murmured. The image needled at him, though, and he moved his shoulder as if to push it away.

"Does Emily have a cat?" Grandma asked, adding salt and pepper to her food.

"Not that I know of."

Grandma furrowed her brows together.

"Are...are you having dreams again?" His mother's face was etched with worry. "Like the ones you had before your surgery?"

"Uh," Nick stuttered, "you mean the ones about that French guy? Jean Claude?"

His mother nodded.

"No."

His grandmother leaned forward. "Who's Jean Claude?"

"A byproduct of a concussion," his father said, giving Nick a look meaning not to go into detail with his grandmother about reincarnation.

"Oh," his grandmother said before going back to her meal. For being such a small person, Grandma had a huge appetite. But they didn't return to the conversation about Stormy, and Nick was glad.

Nick added butter to his potatoes and took a tentative bite—not bad. He ate a carrot.

The voice in his head nudged again. Stormy was part of the fog that surrounded him, much as Jean Claude had crowded him out before. Nick massaged his temples. He needed to get that damned voice out of his head and make those dreams disappear.

"May I be excused? I'm not feeling so hot."

"Of course," his mother said. A frown deepened the crease between her brows.

She reached over to feel his forehead, but he shrugged her off.

"Nice seeing you, Grandma. Sorry, I'm not much company these days." He leaned over and kissed her soft cheek.

"Quite all right, my boy." She reached up and clasped his fingers. "You get your rest, and I'll see you soon. When can you drive?"

Nick looked at his mother, hoping she knew the answer.

"Not for a while." His mom stabbed a carrot with her fork. "Sorry, son." Her apology was accentuated with a sad smile.

Nick climbed the stairs and crawled into his bed, willing his stomach to settle down. All he could see when he closed his eyes was a saw cutting into the flesh of a leg, squirts of blood drenching those helping the surgeon and spilling onto the reddish-brown straw below. The blood of hundreds of men intermingled.

Kentucky blood is the same as Georgia blood. A senseless war with all blood the same color—red.

Chapter 8

"Nick, you have visitors," his mother announced a few days later.

"I don't feel like seeing anyone." He rubbed at the stubble on his face. He hadn't shaved in...he couldn't remember exactly. After a week in the hospital and five days in bed, who could blame him for not wanting to shower or do anything else?

"Even Gary and Tiffany?" she asked.

Gary and Nick met in first grade when they both got detention for throwing rocks on the playground—best buds ever since. And Tiffany was Gary's girlfriend and also a friend of Emily's.

"Yeah, even for us?" Nick heard Tiffany call up as Gary laughed.

"Just for a minute or two." He faked a yawn. "I'm tired." *Not a lie*.

"I'll send them up," his mom called. "Go on!" He could picture her shooing them upstairs, and soon Nick heard the steps creak and protest under Gary's weight.

"Hiya, Nick," Gary said, giving him his signature low whistle. Nick never figured out how Gary had mastered it, a combination of a bird call and a whistle.

"How are you?" Tiffany asked, frowning at him.

Nick raised a hand in greeting and gave them a rueful scowl. "Crappy. Under the weather." Perhaps the longest sentence he'd spoken today.

Gary pulled up the desk chair for Tiffany, and they gathered next to his bed.

"So what's new?" Gary asked. He was never one for words, whereas Tiffany, usually a chatterbox, was strangely quiet today, her large eyes darting around his room and wrinkling her nose.

Maybe my room does smell a bit.

"Nothing, the usual, you know, just a hole in the heart," Nick said in an attempt at humor.

"Yeah, we heard," Gary said, shifting his feet as if talking about it made him uncomfortable.

"How's everyone taking the news?"

"Coach's in mourning," Gary said, crossing his eyes.

Nick laughed at his friend's antics until he felt his stitches tighten. "Hey! I didn't plan it this way."

"Clearly," Gary said giving Nick an exaggerated eye roll and crooked grimace.

Tiffany pointed to the giant envelope Emily had left for him. "Can I look at what people wrote?"

"Sure." He realized he hadn't read any of the messages himself.

She shoved it toward Nick. "From everyone at school. Emily had all of us sign it." Tiffany leaned over and pointed to the names.

Everyone? Nick frowned. His mother said Bryan had signed it. Nick's arch-enemy—the teammate he had tackled by mistake—thinking he was a Nazi soldier. How did someone explain that away without sounding mental? His actions caused them to lose the game.

"Here's mine," Tiffany said. "Get well, Nick," she read. "We miss you and thought you had a big heart before, but it's even better than we thought, patches and all!"

"Thanks." Nick smiled at her.

"Here's what Gary wrote," Tiffany said with a smirk. "Get better, bro!"

Gary shrugged and grimaced toward the floor. "You know I'm not much of a writer and don't like that mushy stuff."

To which Tiffany elbowed Gary. "Not true."

Gary's neck and ears got red, and he said, "I'll help you get caught up on calculus."

"I'll need your help." Nick looked over at the pile of books and folders Emily had left.

Nick yawned.

"We better go, man," Gary said. "I'll come another day and help you get caught up with calculus."

Tiffany leaned over and kissed Nick's cheek. "Bye, Nick. Get better," then quickly added, "Bro!"

Gary slung his arm around Tiffany's shoulders as she giggled. "Come on!" He led her toward the door. "Let's go, Smarty Pants."

Nick raised his arm as they left, set the card aside, and took out his phone. He'd try Cat one more time, but the one-sided texting was getting him nowhere. Perhaps she didn't need his help after all.

—Is everything OK?—

Not expecting an answer, he set his phone aside until he heard a ping.

Finally!

—Can I come over tonight? Homework??—

It was from Emily, and Nick blew out his breath he had been holding.

To Cat: *—I guess U don't need my help.—*

And to Emily: *—Sure!—* Should he add a heart?

He shook his head. Would she think he was flirting? Too soon for heart emojis.

Nick pushed back the quilt and sat at the edge of the bed, mentally considering Emily's visit. Did it mean she still had feelings for him? He felt a tingle when he thought of her pert nose and the way her glasses slipped down, enlarging her already wide compassionate eyes. His heart did a thump-de-da-thump at the thought of Emily's visit.

Chapter 9

Nick had time to think and ponder what had happened during the last few months. As if thinking he was Jean Claude, a French schoolboy, who had fought the Nazis and had loved Chaton, a gypsy girl, wasn't bad enough, Jonathan appeared in his dreams now. Why was he always fighting? He didn't consider himself a fighter. Bryan used his fists to solve problems, but Nick had been taught that words worked better. He guessed both Jean Claude and now Jonathan were pushed into fighting by circumstances beyond their control and not because they liked war.

Nick was tired of dreaming and remembering war and wanted the soldiers to go away and leave him alone. Would Jean Claude keep bugging him? Or would this Jonathan guy and Jean Claude gang up on him?

Only Jonathan came tonight—a dirty, ragged man with a beard and a disheveled appearance in a blue army uniform, all tattered. Nick looked down at the hand that rested on the threadbare uniform—square, rough fingers with dirt-encrusted nails. He was Nick, and Nick was Jonathan. The thought seemed to lodge in Nick's head.

"No, not his leg," I begged. I couldn't help myself from crying out for the man. "How can he work his farm with only one leg?"

They surrounded a man with a red/purple streak

from his knee to the groin. The man groaned in agony and tried to reach his leg, but we held his hands down. The hospital tent used a scarred table for the operation. At one time, the table had hosted family meals. Now, they were carving something far different than a roast.

"If it doesn't come off, he won't live past the gangrene," the surgeon said. We called the surgeon Sawbones because he used a saw to cut through men's bones to sever a leg or an arm from gangrene, a poison from the bullets lodged in the body—the evil black or red monster.

I shivered.

"Now hold him still," the surgeon said. "Steady, steady," he whispered. "Give him something to bite on so he doesn't take his tongue clean off."

"Can't we give him something? Morphine? Opium?" I asked, the bile rising to my throat.

"Ran out days ago."

I remembered the soldier who had taken all the opium tincture for his suicide, leaving nothing for the rest.

I gave the man a bullet to bite before grasping his leg.

"No," the soldier screamed as the saw bit into his flesh. "I can't stand the pain!" He arched his back, trying to pull away from the hands holding him.

The surgeon gripped the saw and, with a determined set to his mouth, began to saw through skin, muscle, and bone, blood spurting.

I tore my eyes away as the wound gaped open, blood spilling out and the white of the bone exposed. I turned and vomited onto the sawdust floor. One more vile smell to mingle with the odors of metallic blood, bodily fluids, disease, and the stench of death—a nauseating cauldron of misery.

Another man ran over after the surgeon was done with a red-hot poker and applied it to the bloody stump. Thankfully the man had lost consciousness from the pain. The stump sizzled and smoked like bacon on a griddle.

I retched again and rubbed at my thigh. My leg had a minie ball lodged in it, and I watched the infection grow each day. I didn't let anyone see it—no one. Was losing a leg my fate as well? Right now, an angry red circle marked the spot.

"Are you all right, son?"

I squinted at the figure dressed in black—a minister—a man with kind eyes and calloused hands holding a Bible. "Your name?" he asked, patting my shoulder.

"Jonathan," I gasped. "I can't believe the brutality of war."

"I will pray for you, Jonathan."

"Pray I can go home to my family." I desperately wanted to go home. The war had aged me far past my twenty-five years.

"I will do so."

When he left, I turned to vomit again, but nothing came up, and I gagged over and over. And if the red monster took my life, what of my wife and children? Who would take care of them? If I returned from the war, I'd have one leg. I missed Emeline—my pert, sassy, fierce wife. She had borne both our children with nary a peep and had helped me work the fields with a babe strapped to her back. I imagined we'd do fine even if I had one leg.

They finished the surgeries for the day, and I stumbled outside for fresh air. It began to rain, and I let the warm water stream down my body washing away the stench of the hospital, washing away my fears of the future.

Water soaked my threadbare uniform. When the war between the Confederate and the Union started, my uniform had been clean, and the buttons gleamed. Now many months later, I had holes in both elbows and was missing some buttons. We were winning the war, but the list of dead men was posted in the camp. I scanned the list for familiar names—the Johnson brothers were both casualties. What would become of their families?

I let my shoulders slump forward and hands hang down until a movement caught my eye. A dark shape huddled near the tent's flap, and two eyes glowed in the gloom—a drenched kitten.

"Here, kitty, kitty," I coaxed.

Moving cautiously, the cat came closer. I stooped and held out my hand. "It's okay. I won't hurt you."

The cat was almost to my side.

"Let's get you dried off and out of the rain." I scooped her up and cradled her in my arms as I went back to my cot and the relative warmth of the tent.

When dried, she was the color of the storm clouds. "I think you are a stormy cat. I'll call you Stormy. Would you like that?"

Her answer stayed mainly in my head. Yes, she liked the name, Stormy.

Chapter 10

January 15, 1865
My darling Emeline:
I got your last letter and cherished each word. And was in better spirits after having read it. I'm glad the girls are growing along with the garden. I picture them with their smiling faces and dream about them and you at night.

You ask of the war. What can I say, the battle is endless and tiring, and both sides have significant casualties. We're camped at Virginney, waiting for the Rebels to find us. I'll say this for the Rebs, they are like a fox in the hen house, always looking for a means. I had hoped to be home by now and bring in the crops, but sadly that's not the way of war.

I've been assigned to the hospital tent because of my animal husbandry. But tending men and beasts are far different. A poultice for a hock is far different when a man must lose an arm or leg. I see the streaks of red evilness run up men's limbs and pray for them knowing it might mean the end. The preachers are plumb worn out, tending to the sick and dying. Our supplies of drugs and bandages have almost run out. We make do, but the pain these men must endure is wrenching. I took a minie ball in the leg, but the red devil hasn't taken me.

I found a stray kitten who has taken to me and goes with me as I tend to the sick. I'm teased about having a

cat for a girlfriend. You don't mind, do you?
   My love always for you, Sophia, and Anne.
   I miss you all something fierce! Yours, Jonathan

Chapter 11

Dr. Sara Beth Patar—Dr. Garson's referral—was a psychologist and would help him sort out his feelings, Nick guessed.

This morning, Nick and his mother waited in Dr. Patar's reception area. Nick had been to more doctor's visits since his heart surgery than all the other fifteen years combined. The waiting areas all took on the same monotonous tone—neutral furniture, magazines, and tasteful, nondescript artwork that looked like someone had splashed paint on a canvas and called it good. Dr. Patar's waiting area was the same.

His mother squeezed his hand. "How are you feeling today?"

Wasn't Dr. Patar supposed to ask those kinds of questions? "Okay, I guess."

His mother studied him. Their eyes mirrored each other, Nick had noticed, brown with almost black irises and a ring of golden brown around the edge. She smiled back at him. Could his mother see into his soul as easily as Cat had?

"I just want my Nick back," she said and squeezed his hand.

"What do you mean?"

She paused and licked her lips before responding. "The Nick that was into school and sports." She sighed. "I just don't see that anymore in you."

Nick tilted his head to the side. He guessed she was right. "It's been a strange year," he said.

Could he go through what he had and be "normal" again? His father said experience was the best teacher.

"Nicholas?" A nurse called his name as she opened a door.

"Do you want me to go with you?" his mother asked as he struggled out of the chair.

"It might be better if I go alone." He pushed himself up. "I'll fill you in later."

His mom slumped back and nodded.

Dr. Patar was different than Dr. Sims. She was even taller, like a basketball player or model.

"Nicholas." She held out her hand to him.

He shook her cool long fingers. "Call me, Nick, please."

"All right, Nick," Dr. Patar said, indicating he should sit. "Let's get acquainted."

He took the offered chair, suddenly feeling nervous.

Dr. Patar noticed his hunched shoulders. "Nothing hardcore today, Nick. We're going to get to know each other." She smiled. "I want to know Nick Dupont."

He inclined his head to the folder on her desk with his name on the label. "Isn't everything in there?" He doubted he could explain who he was. He didn't know for sure himself.

She opened the folder and took out two sheets of paper. The print was tiny. "This tells me you are sixteen years old and a junior at Laketon High. You had a heart defect repaired and are now depressed. Do you want to know your height and weight too?"

"No."

"Tell me about Nick from your point of view then. What do you like to do? What are your hobbies? Sports? Books you've read…"

Where to start? "You already know I'm a junior," Nick mumbled. He picked at a loose thread on his pants. "Used to be a pretty good student."

"Used to be?"

"Yeah." He looked up. "Grades did a nosedive this year." He gestured with his hand pointing down. "I used to play football." He paused for her reaction, but she remained quiet. "I guess football was my hobby too. My dad played pro football for the Lions, and I thought I wanted to follow in his footsteps…" He cleared his throat. "I'm not sure about playing football anymore."

"How does that make you feel?"

She wasn't using visualization to probe his soul. No, she was interested in his thoughts and feelings—a more intrusive probing.

"I feel lost like I'm walking along a trail and have no idea where I'm going."

"And when did your lost feeling start? Was it after your surgery?"

"Before. But it's complicated."

She laughed. "Isn't everything?"

"I just want to figure out who I am again."

"And how would you like to be?" she asked.

"Happy. Predictable. Following my Christian upbringing."

"And you're none of those things now?"

"Bingo." Nick gave her a thumbs-up.

"If you had a magic wand, what would you change to make your problems disappear?" she asked.

"I'd invent a time machine and go back before I met Cat."

Or before he was even born and changed the course of events.

"Pardon," Dr. Patar said. "Did you say cat? As in a feline?"

"No, Cat is a person. Her abbreviated name. Catherine Anne Thomlinson—Cat for short."

"Sorry, please go on. Why do you wish you could go back before you met Cat?"

"It started at the beginning of the school year when we were assigned as work partners."

The doc took notes as he talked.

Nick continued, "We were to do a research project about WWII, and she said she wanted to 'start where we had left off.' " He gestured with air quotes. "I didn't understand what the heck she was talking about. So when she said, 'I had left her to die,' I felt terrible."

"You left her to die? Where?"

"An internment camp." He paused before adding, "During WWII."

The heavy silence weighed between them as Nick let his words sink in. The doc stopped writing, her pen poised over the paper. Finally, she glanced up with a frown. "You left her to die during that war?" Dr. Patar did a head shake as if she was trying to dislodge a stuck thought. "How old are you, Nick?"

"Sixteen. Both Cat and I are sixteen."

"Did you think such a thing was possible with the war being seventy-some years ago?"

"She believed we were 'souls' who knew each other from a different time."

"You didn't believe that?"

"Not exactly."

"Doesn't sound like you're sure of your beliefs," she said, leaning forward.

"I guess not. My parents told me some things that happened when I was little."

"Such as?"

"I sometimes talked in French and told them about being a French soldier."

"While that's unusual, it's not uncommon."

"Really?" He sat forward and raised his brows.

"Certainly," Dr. Patar said. "People with head trauma sometimes speak a different language."

"I was only five when I told them about being a French soldier."

"You may have had some trauma early in your life."

Nick shrugged. "I did fall out of a tree when I was a kid and have a scar on my chest."

"When did you start to play football?" she asked.

Nick chuckled. "As soon as I could walk, I think. My parents said I only wanted to hold a football and practice throwing it and tackling my stuffed animals."

"We're learning that helmets aren't adequate protection against head trauma."

"I guess I'm screwed." Nick threw up his hands.

"Not necessarily." She folded her arms.

"How do people learn to speak a different language?" Nick changed the subject. "I've never had French. My parents don't speak it. I don't know anyone who speaks French."

"The brain is an amazing organ capable of picking up all sorts of things."

"You don't think I'm crazy?" he asked, suddenly

feeling hope.

She smiled at him. "Hardly."

"Can you help me?" he asked, splaying his fingers as if stretching them.

"To the best of my abilities."

He gave her a tentative smile and blew out the breath he didn't know he was holding. Finally, some help! If the voices stopped talking to him, then maybe, just maybe, he could return to "normal."

"Let's start when you fell out of the tree and began talking about the French soldier."

"Do you think the two things are connected?" Nick asked, the pulse in his neck thudding in expectation.

She nodded.

"I thought I was some guy named Jean Claude who was buried in France."

"And you spoke French?"

"Yes, a little. My kindergarten report card said I spoke to the class in French."

Dr. Patar nodded nonjudgmentally and gestured for him to continue.

"When researching our project, I read a couple of passages about the war written in French."

"What you're describing has a name."

"It's a real thing?" Nick leaned closer to Dr. Patar. "Cat said my past life soul was speaking."

"Dissociative Identity is a real mental disorder."

"Dissociative Identity?" Nick repeated. The unfamiliar word was a tongue twister.

"Yes." She nodded. "People having more than one identity."

"So, I can be fixed?" Nick secretly smirked—Jonathan and the talking cat would go away.

She sighed. "Mainly, with counseling," Dr. Patar said. "There's a treatment center in Grand Rapids that may be able to help you."

"Oh? There isn't a pill I can take?" Nick frowned.

"I'm afraid not." As she talked, she moved around the pens and notes on her desk.

"We saw a Regression Therapist who helped me call up my 'past soul.' "

"Interesting," she said. "Like I said, not unusual. Robert Louis Stevenson wrote 'Dr. Jekyll and Mr. Hyde' about multiple personalities, and there have been several movies made about the disorder—*Three Faces of Eve* and *Sybil*."

"People know about this kind of stuff?" Nick asked, happy for a label but unhappy he had a mental disorder. That label gnawed at him. He wasn't perfect. Nobody was perfect, but he didn't want a "mental disorder" hanging over his head.

"Yes, we can use cognitive behavior therapy to treat it. And even hypnosis can help. I can guide you so you can integrate each personality into your life. We call those other personalities 'alters'—alternate personalities." She stopped. "Are there others?"

Nick nodded.

She continued, "How many?"

"Two so far." He cleared his throat. "You don't think I'm crazy?" he asked again.

"Of course not."

"And Cat?"

Dr. Patar shook her head. "I'm not treating her."

"So two people with personality disorders…" Nick paused. "Found each other?"

"Stranger things have happened." She gave him a

tentative smile and looked up at the clock. "Come next week, and we'll talk more."

Nick grasped her smile as a lifeline and returned the gesture. Finally some help. If Cat was still in Laketon he could have shared his news, but she hadn't responded to any of his texts. The —*Help me! Please!*— text still needled him. Was Cat playing games or was she in real trouble? He'd need to move forward without her.

Chapter 12

Nick left Dr. Patar and returned to his mother, who booked another appointment for the following week. "All finished?"

"Come on, let's go." Nick waved his mom toward the door. "I'm starving, and I'll tell you about it in the car." Yes, he was hungry, and part of the heavy weight on his chest had lessened, but was having a real disorder better than the mumbo jumbo about being reincarnated? He decided—at least he liked it better than going against his Christian teachings.

They settled into the car, and she turned to him. "I can tell by your face you're feeling better." She put the car in reverse and backed out of the parking space.

"A little. The doctor didn't think I was crazy. It may be due to a concussion or other trauma."

His mother paused and ran her tongue over her lips. "I know they are discovering all kinds of interesting things about head trauma." His mother checked the car's mirrors as she eased into the traffic.

"She thinks I may have something called Dissociative Identity Disorder." His tongue stumbled over the word dissociative. "I might have two personalities," he explained. "Jean Claude, the French guy, and Nick Dupont." And someone named Jonathan but telling his mother any more would only increase her concern.

"Hmm," his mother said as she took the exit for Laketon.

Nick glanced over at her before continuing, "She told me that the Jekyll and Hyde book was written about it, and a couple of movies were made about women with multiple personalities."

"Sure." His mother tapped her palm on the steering wheel. "*Three Faces of Eve* and *Sybil*. How is something like this treated?"

"More therapy." Nick shrugged. "She told me there aren't any drugs for it. I want to read more about it when we get home." His stomach gurgled in reply.

His mother laughed. "I heard that! What do you want to eat?"

"Just swing by a drive-thru and get me a chicken sandwich."

"A chicken sandwich?" His mother quirked a brow at him.

"Yeah."

"I've never known you to order a chicken sandwich."

Beef still made him nauseous.

He scowled. "I'm off beef. The hospital killed my appetite for it." A lie but a plausible excuse his mother would buy.

"Your wish is my command," his mother said. Nick could tell by her light tone she felt better with a name for his dual personality—him, too.

It would be good not to have his mother hovering around him, worry on her face. He would have time to think about how to put his life back on track and salvage what he could. His parents' haggard looks told him he had been a huge disappointment to them

51

through this whole thing. Their perfect son vanished because of an encounter with a new student at school.

Nick's mother reached over and grasped his fingers. "Are you upset by what she told you?"

"I don't know if I'm happy or upset."

His mother found a fast-food restaurant, ordered him the sandwich which he ate as they drove. The discussion about his disorder was over for now.

Once at home Nick went to his bedroom, sat on the bed, pulled out his cell phone, and typed: —*I'm not reincarnated. You got it wrong.*—

Cat never responded, though, but maybe she couldn't. He hadn't heard back from her after her cryptic message for help. What if something had happened to her? He might never know and shook away his ambivalent feelings for her. Nick yawned widely before closing his eyes for a cat nap—a slip of the tongue or in this case, his thoughts.

Later Nick got out of bed and tentatively stretched his arms, feeling the pull on his chest. He tugged on the collar of his tee shirt and examined his scar in the mirror. The line on his skin was getting lighter, the skin puckered but not bruised, and the sutures had dissolved away.

Nick debated between going downstairs for a snack or doing some research. The vacuum cleaner was running downstairs, and he was still full from the chicken sandwich. He'd skip the snack for the time being.

He sat at his desk and turned on his laptop and typed in the words "Dissociative Identity Disorder."

Dissociative Identity Disorder (DID)—having more than one identity caused by drug use, illness, trauma, or pretend play.

Nick frowned. Falling out of a tree caused him to have multiple personalities? He used his palms to scrub at his eyes. The definition was still the same.

He continued reading: *DID is a mental disorder characterized by at least two distinct and relatively enduring identities or dissociated personality states.*

Well, that certainly pertained to him, but why did Jean Claude or Jonathan mainly visit him in his dreams? There were those two times during the football game, he mistakenly thought the Nazis were on the field and he attacked Bryan.

Nick rolled his eyes remembering that game and the crap he got from Bryan over his confusion.

DID is one of the most controversial psychiatric disorders, he read. There was no clear agreement on diagnostic criteria or treatment. *Diagnosis is often difficult, as the illness is frequently associated with other mental disorders.*

Still, doubts nagged him. Did he want to know the truth? He tapped his fingers. Yes and no. Did he want the diagnosis of DID? Or to believe in reincarnation? Neither option seemed good.

He drummed his fingers on the desk until he heard his parents' voices in the living room and went downstairs to talk to them.

"Hi, son, what have you been doing? Catching up on homework?" his father asked.

"Researching DID."

"Your mother mentioned that." His father frowned and leaned forward.

His mother muted the TV. "What have you found out?"

"Besides falling out of the tree, what other trauma did I suffer?"

His father cleared his throat. "Your grandfather's death was hard on you."

Nick frowned and licked his lips. He knew his grandfather had died but couldn't remember the circumstances.

"He had cancer. Right?"

His parents turned toward each other and frowned. When Nick's father placed his palms on his knees, a gesture Nick knew to be his "we're going to have a lecture or sermon," he took a deep breath.

"You don't remember?" his father asked.

"No," Nick said with a shake of his head.

"It was awful," his mother said, tears in her eyes.

"Grandpa was diagnosed with cancer and took all his pills—" his father said quietly.

Did he mean Grandpa killed himself? Nick could hardly believe that. Not Grandpa. Not his hero! The D-Day soldier who fought the Germans. Who told stories about the war that made Nick want to learn more about history? Why would he do something like that? And why hadn't Nick remembered?

Nick ran his teeth over his bottom lip and whispered, "I don't remember that." He gulped back tears that pricked at the backs of his eyes. How awful for Grandpa to have felt that sad and end his life. Nick couldn't imagine getting to that point. "But he was a hero, wasn't he?"

"Oh, yes!" his mother said. "I think he took all those pills because of cancer in his pancreas."

"Pancreatic cancer is often fatal," his father said.

Nick sniffed. "I just want to remember him as my

hero."

She reached over and grasped his hand. "He's your hero." She bowed her head. "He's my hero too."

"But does he get to go to Heaven?"

His father frowned. "Why would you say that?"

Nick racked his brains to remember where he had heard that. "I dunno."

"He was a good man. He went to Heaven, I'm sure," his father said, his voice reassuring and calm.

Nick chewed his bottom lip. Some of the heaviness in his soul lifted, and he felt lighter knowing his grandfather was in Heaven where he belonged.

Chapter 13

March 21, 1865
My Dearest Jonathan:
We were glad to get your last letter. Garrett's boy, Abraham, helped bring the crops in. A sorry sight as half the corn was trampled by the Rebs that came this way. We hid in the cellar, and they didn't harm us. They robbed us of the meat we had smoked, most of my laying chickens, my sacks of flour and sugar, and even my last jars of preserves. I had the presence of mind to hide some things in the barn behind the corn crib so we won't starve. A few of the chickens took to the trees when the commotion began.

Sophia is teaching Anne to read. Your sister brought them a book from England—Alice in Wonderland. The girls have been enjoying Alice's exploits with the white rabbit and talking cat.

The girls are growing so fast that I had to cut down some of my old dresses to make new frocks for Sophia as Anne is wearing her castoff dresses. I was able to trade a side of bacon for some shoes so we wouldn't go around barefooted.

You have always had a kind heart toward animals. But a cat as a sweetheart? Really? Jonathan! But I don't mind.

We are so hoping you could be with us soon and are praying for your safe return to us.
My everlasting love, Emeline

Chapter 14

Before Emily came over the next night after school, Nick showered, changed into clean clothes and pushed the pile of dirty laundry into the closet, and closed the door so Emily couldn't see the mess. And for good measure, he sprayed air freshener around the door.

His mother came in and sniffed. "What do I smell?"

"Just cleaning up before Em gets here."

"I've come for your laundry." She paused and looked around before going to the closet and gathering the dirty clothes.

He was looking forward to seeing Emily. With her back in his life, he could concentrate on being Nick Dupont again, not some long-dead soldier. Or soldiers—plural. And, he had a diagnosis now, too, that made sense and not something weird or spooky like reincarnation.

Emily arrived, and they sat at his desk. "You look better today," she said, turning to study him.

"Do you want to see my scar?" he asked.

"Can I?" she asked, leaning forward.

He pulled down the neck of his shirt for her to see the pink line down his breastbone.

"Wow," she said before her jaw went slack with surprise.

"Yup opened up my chest and put a patch on my

heart." He let go of the collar.

They sat silently until Nick cleared his throat. "I'm sorry what happened at the homecoming dance, Em."

She looked at him, assessing his sincerity. He truly meant it. He was glad Cat had gone, and he could be Nick again.

Today, Emily wore sneakers with hearts on them. A good omen? Or the luck of the draw? Nick wanted to believe she was inadvertently sending him a message—a green light!

"It's good to have you back," Emily finally replied. "I still don't understand what happened."

He moved his head, turning over possible explanations.

"You said someone else was kissing her." She quirked her brow at him. "Were you two acting?"

Acting? Kind of. They were portraying someone else...

"I guess you could say that. The doctor I saw said people with my disorder sometimes play act."

"What disorder do you have?" Her brow furrowed, and her eyes narrowed suspiciously.

He reached over and squeezed her fingers.

"They think I have Dissociative Identity Disorder—DID—from head trauma."

"When did that happen?" she demanded.

"When I was a kid."

"Really?"

Her fingers were soft and warm. Nick wanted to hold her hand longer.

"Thank you for coming to see me after what I did," he said. "I'm sorry. Thank you for believing I'm not a bad person."

"I don't think you're bad," she said. "I think you got sidetracked by that girl."

"I know. She's gone now."

"Yes." Emily pulled her hand back. "I hope she stays in Oregon."

"Me too." If Cat did return, he would push her out of his life. Nope, Cat wouldn't come between them again, he determined. She had been ignoring his texts. Had she been teasing him with her "help me" message? Cat was hard to figure out.

"What do you think she wanted exactly?" Emily asked.

"I think she was searching for answers." Nick raised an eyebrow. "I found out she was adopted and moved a lot. I felt sorry for her."

Emily inclined her head as she contemplated Nick's last sentence. "You might be right."

Nick's mother knocked on the door, and it popped open. "Emily, would you like to stay for dinner?"

Nick looked at her and smiled. Emily smiled too, making her brows wiggle.

"Let me check with my mother." Emily pulled out her phone and stepped into the hall.

"What are we having?" Nick asked his mother, while Emily called her parents to tell them she was staying for dinner.

"Chicken." He lifted his nose and sniffed the air. Yup, fowl tonight. Good, no more beef. The thought of bloodied meat sickened him, and he frowned.

"Sound okay to you?" his mother asked. "Only chicken and fish from now on," she promised, patting her stomach. "I could probably stand to lose a few pounds."

Nick shook his head. "You're perfect the way you are, Mom."

"Thank you."

"Dessert?" he asked.

"Hmm, what would you like?" she asked.

"Salt pork cake?" Nick asked although he didn't know why. His mother made chocolate cake and strawberry shortcake. Now he couldn't recall ever eating a salt pork cake, although he could taste it in his mouth, sweetness and warmth filling his belly.

"That's an odd request," she said. "And kinda disgusting!" She gagged.

"Is it?"

"I've never made a salt pork cake in my life! What's in it?"

Nick narrowed his eyes and pictured the list of ingredients that went into the cake. "Pork fat. Baking soda. Flour. Raisins, cloves, cinnamon, nuts, and dates."

"Sounds like a fruitcake," his mother said.

"It is." He pictured a slice of the cake showing the nuts, dates, and raisins. "Did Grandma make that kind of cake?"

"You can ask her yourself." She shrugged, her face breaking into a smile. "Grandma's here!"

When Emily finished talking to her mother, they went downstairs to join Grandma for dinner. Grandma began smiling at the sight of Emily.

"My lands! Emily! So glad to see you!" Grandma said, reaching out her arm to them. "Nick finally came to his senses."

Emily inclined her head. "I'm helping him get caught up in school." She kissed Grandma on the cheek.

"You ready to go back to school?" Grandma asked Nick.

Was he? The thought was neutral, neither good nor bad. "I think I am."

"I don't want my favorite grandson left behind."

"I'm your only grandson." He hugged her.

"As I said, 'my favorite one.' " She smirked but patted his hand.

Nick was secretly pleased by her remarks. "Did you ever make me a salt pork cake?"

"That's a strange question," Grandma said, tipping her head back as if searching for answers on the ceiling.

"It's fruitcake," Nick's mom explained.

"Why didn't you just say fruitcake?" she admonished.

"Don't know." Nick shrugged while Emily smirked at him.

"Dinner's served," Nick's father said, wiping his hands on the apron he wore.

His father placed honey and butter on the table with some cornbread.

No sorghum? He frowned at the honey.

"Am I missing something?" his father asked, noting Nick's confused grimace. "Nick?"

"Um…"

"You love honey and butter on cornbread," his father prompted.

"Do I?" Nick asked.

"Of course." His father motioned for Emily to sit next to Nick.

"I've a hankering for sorghum." Nick's mind was playing tricks on him. Sorghum was in the wrong context. It was from before, not now. He didn't think he had ever tasted sorghum as Nick Dupont. And too, Emily peered at him strangely.

That was all wrong, and he knew it. He had sorghum when he ate Johnny cakes.

"Sorghum," Grandma said, rolling it around her tongue. "Now, that's an old-fashioned term I haven't heard in a while!"

"Are you okay?" his father asked, reaching out as if to check Nick's temperature.

Nick moved away from his father's hand and didn't know what to say. "Must have been something I read," he mumbled.

His parents made small talk with Emily and Grandma. Nick nodded and tried to act interested in their thoughts about the weather, what was happening at school, and at Grandma's senior apartment complex.

"Nick? Everything taste okay?" his mother asked, frowning at his half-eaten food.

"Sure! Tastes great," he said, turning his attention to his dinner.

After Grandma and Emily left and Nick was alone in his bedroom, he pulled out his phone to message Cat.

—*This is my last text. Goodbye.*—

Chapter 15

I surveyed the line of men on stretchers as we prepared to leave West Virginia. We would follow the army and drop off the wounded at the nearest hospital. Some wounded could walk, some were carried, and still a few limped along with crutches or canes. Stormy followed me, always at my side. I scooped her up and placed her next to the man I would help carry. I hoisted my end of the stretcher after nodding to the man with one arm and one leg.

"Leave me behind," the man croaked. "Just let me die." He stroked Stormy with his hand.

"We're taking you to the hospital."

" 'Tis no use," he said quietly and closed his eyes while keeping a hand on Stormy.

Stormy was a comfort to many men in the hospital tent.

We sang as we marched along with our burden— "Home! Sweet Home!" The wounded, if they could, joined in. I'm on my way—the tune made me miss my Emeline and daughters something fierce! I recalled her last letter asking me if I was well. A much-read letter folded tenderly in my pocket. I had studied each word by the kerosene lantern, imaging her writing it by the glow of the fire after the young'uns were abed. Was I well? I had taken a bullet in the leg too, but I was better than the man on the stretcher. Could any man really say he was fine after watching soldiers shoot each other at close range? The fallen were left to rot after their boots, munitions, and jackets were wrestled from their stiff bodies. The rivers ran red with blood—a gruesome sight.

The following morning, Nick got out of bed, half expecting to see a long and winding road. He peered out the window at paved streets with modern cars and not a red dirt road—the crimson dust seeping onto people, clothing, and animals until everything glowed of freshly let blood. And he was humming—a song he knew but didn't. Was he humming, "When Johnny comes marching home again?"

Nick felt chills crawl up his spine, clamped his lips together, stopped humming, and surveyed his bedroom. He wasn't in the place of his dreams—the hospital tent—only an unmade bed, dresser, bookshelves, and desk. He held out his hand and studied it. The man in his dreams had dirty, rough hands, but Nick's were clean. But somewhere in his DNA, he had morphed into Jonathan and back again—a man so different from Nick's current life.

Nick had awoken, determined to tackle calculus. Instead, his thoughts went back to *marching down a dusty road, either side littered with bodies of those who had died on their journey toward Virginia. It was sobering to see in death the soldiers of the two armies left side by side. Did Jesus care if they wore gray or blue? I forced my gaze toward the road ahead and not what we had left behind.*

"You up?" Nick's mother called, the creaking stairs announcing her approach.

The Union's ragtag army vanished, and it took

Nick a moment to clear his head. How could men do that to each other?

Nick massaged his thigh, easing away the unexplained tenderness. "Homework," he panted. The short bursts of breath surprised him, almost as if Nick had run up the stairs or carried a heavy burden.

"Breakfast?" she asked.

"Later." And when he heard her retreat down the steps, he pulled up his pajama bottoms to study his leg. Nick blinked, half expecting to see an ugly sore on his thigh. He had seen gangrene crawl up a man's leg or arm, sending out tentacles of red, purple, or black as it ate away at the flesh. Had he ever seen such a wound or sore before? He realized he had and pushed Jonathan away.

"Leave me alone," he muttered, scrubbing at his sleep-encrusted eyes.

Jonathan retreated, although Nick knew he lurked in the shadows. Nick was determined to do his schoolwork. With his mouth in a grim, determined line, he sat down and took out calculus and studied the directions. *Show the tangent line to the graph of a function at a given point.*

He bent his head and began figuring out the tangent line, chewing his lip in concentration. They had not followed a tangent line in the army. No, the path was curved and bumpy. Again, he banished the thoughts and tried to concentrate on the straight black line on the paper. With a mind of its own, it moved from blue to gray and back again.

He put down his pencil. How could he get his work done if he kept remembering the past?

Minnie hopped up on his bed and surveyed him,

her eyes bright and unblinking. He reached out, scratching her head, and in response, she raised her paw and batted his hand away before jumping onto his desk, sitting on top of his textbook.

"You know you can't forget about me, Jonathan. I'm your cat," a tiny voice in his head said.

"I don't know who you are, Stormy." Nick shook his head, trying to shake away that voice.

"You know who I am. Who do I remind you of?"

Who did the cat remind him of? No one. Then a smudged and hazy gray image took shape. *Go away*!

Minnie blinked at him and jumped back to the bed. Nick's heart beat quicker as he forcefully silenced the cat's voice and once again, turned back to his homework.

Chapter 16

Nick's mother drove him to Dr. Patar's office, and instead of staying, she dropped him off, saying, "Are you sure you'll be fine if I don't go with you?"

He scowled at her. "Mom…"

"I know. I know." She moved her hands in a surrender gesture.

"You have to wait in the lobby anyway."

"True!" She blew him a kiss before leaving.

"Hi, Nick," Dr. Patar greeted him. "Why don't you get comfortable, and we can talk further."

Nick moved around in the chair to find a place that suited him.

"Have you had time to think about what we discussed last week?"

That was all he thought about!

"I looked up some things on the internet," Nick offered.

"Good, now you know what we're up against."

Nick suddenly became interested in a worn part of his jeans and picked at a thread. "I talked to my parents, and I guess I had a pretty big trauma in my life."

Dr. Patar frowned at her notes. "More than just falling out of a tree?"

"Yes." He took a deep breath. "My grandfather committed suicide, and I forgot about it."

"Were you close?"

"He was my hero," Nick said quietly. He thought back to their time together. Fishing at the Lake Michigan channel and looking through Grandpa's pictures about his fellow soldiers in Normandy.

"That would certainly constitute a traumatic event," Dr. Patar said.

Nick tore his attention from those memories to what Dr. Patar was saying.

"He was sick." Nick cleared his throat. "Cancer. He took all his pills and ended it."

"That is terrible," she agreed.

A long pause followed, and he waited for her to continue.

She took a deep breath and said, "There's been some research into using selective serotonin reuptake inhibitors for DID." She folded her hands on the desk. "The drug can be used for post-trauma stress disorder and may help with your alters. You said they were both soldiers. And your grandfather was a soldier, too, so that may be the connection. I can prescribe it, and we'll see if it helps."

"What else can we do?" Nick fidgeted with his fingers. He was already taking drugs for his heart and depression.

"We can try hypnosis to return to what you remember about your grandfather and see if that helps."

"And if it doesn't?"

"We'll try something else. Sometimes knowing you have these alternate personalities will help you decide how to act in a certain situation."

"So knowing about them is good?"

"It's a start." She licked her lips. "I probably should have a session with you and your parents and explain what DID is."

"Okay." Nick hung his head. Another burden for his parents to shoulder.

"I'll set something up with your mother before you leave," Dr. Patar said, pushing back her chair and standing.

"She dropped me off. Should I have her call you?"

"Yes."

Once in the car, he relayed the message to his mother.

Chapter 17

When Nick and his mother returned home, Nick tackled more homework and worked diligently until the house phone rang downstairs, causing him to stop and wonder who was calling.

"Coach is coming for a visit," his mother shouted.

Nick could imagine her standing at the bottom of the stairs, cupping her mouth to project her voice to his bedroom. He frowned. He couldn't picture a coach—only a vision of a man wearing a uniform and holding a pistol. Nick's gaze bounced around the room, resting on his football trophies. Ah, a football coach, not a man with a gun.

The creaking of the steps alerted him the man was coming for him, and his breath remained stuck.

"Knock. Knock," a voice said. "Nick?" The body accompanying the voice was nothing like he had imagined. Coach wore a tracksuit and a baseball cap with the Laketon Lancer's logo.

"Hi." Nick gasped, happy he imagined the wrong person. But it was always confusing to wonder what people would appear before him.

Who was he? Nick? Jean Claude? Or this new person, Jonathan?

"I can't stay long, but I just wanted to see you for a few minutes." Coach came into the room. "I wanted to see how my favorite football player is doing."

Nick managed a rueful smile. "I'm not sure football is in my future."

"Your mother said you could probably play again."

"I'm keeping my options open," Nick said, swiveling the chair so he could see Coach.

"I understand that," Coach said.

"I'm sure I've been a huge disappointment to you this year," Nick said. "And I'm sorry."

"Not true. We had no idea of your hidden heart defect." He pulled something from his pocket and handed him a card. "From the guys." Coach patted Nick's shoulder. "We'll talk again when you're better."

Nick wasn't sure he'd ever be well, but he managed a rueful smile before flopping down on the bed after Coach left. He picked up the card and examined his name scrawled on the front. He wondered what kind of messages the team had sent him.

Nick drew out the card. On the front was a picture of a basset hound with a mournful look wearing a hot water bottle on his head. Nick opened the card. The names were written into the small space.

Sentiments like: "get well," "see you soon," "hurry back," etc. Bryan had signed his name but wrote nothing. Gary had drawn a hapless-looking football player on a stretcher with a frown and the message— "We need you!"

Nick doubted they needed him. They needed the old him, not the new one with personalities and past lives coming out of his ears.

Chapter 18

The following week, Nick and his parents were scheduled to see Dr. Patar. The week had flown by with Gary helping with calculus, and Emily helping him in his other subjects.

"Are you about ready for our appointment?" his mother called.

Nick turned over, sniffing the breakfast smells in the air: coffee, frying eggs, and butter.

He made a face, not because of the smells but having to see another doctor. He should be used to these interruptions to his days.

Nick eased himself out of bed, shuffled to the bathroom, showered, changed, and now he stood smoothing down his jeans, the waist sagging from weight loss. "Coming."

He walked down the steps slowly—at least he wasn't clutching the handrail in a death grip anymore. He was recovering his strength. If he got the go-ahead from Dr. Garson, he could return to school.

His mother appraised his descent. "Feeling like your old self?" she asked.

"I'm about eighty percent. I want to go back to school."

She raised her brows.

School would keep his mind occupied, and he could see Emily. If all went according to plan, he would wiggle his way into Emily's heart again.

"Best thing I'd heard today," she said, her voice light.

They got into his mother's car, driving to Dr. Patar's office in silence. "Your dad's going to meet us."

"I don't think a meeting is necessary." Nick continued looking out the window at the sights flipping by, not really seeing the trees, cars and trucks, or houses. A tingle pricked at his stomach. Why that feeling—a feeling of dread.

"Dr. Patar wanted to talk to us." She wiggled her fingers on the steering wheel.

"Okay." Nick shrugged. "But I think it's a waste of your time. This diagnosis is something I'm going to have to figure out."

"True, but we want to be as supportive as possible."

"Fair."

When his father arrived, they all trooped into Dr. Patar's office. "Thank you for coming today to discuss Nick and his possible disorder."

Nick's dad leaned forward. "Possible disorder?"

"There is no test to determine exactly why Nick has these alter personalities. The 'alters' as we call them are often a reaction to some stress or trauma or even alcohol."

Nick's mother inhaled loudly and coughed. "Alcohol?"

Nick thought back to the start of the school year when he drank more. Had that contributed to this disorder?

"I believe Nick has these alter personalities because of some stresses and trauma in his life," Dr.

Patar repeated.

"We live a pretty bland and boring life," his father interjected.

"I think his grandfather's death"—Dr. Patar glanced down at her notes and put her finger on something before continuing—"and perhaps some head trauma from falling out of the tree and football injuries to the head have contributed to what he's going through."

"How do you treat this, Dr. Patar?" Nick's father demanded.

"Unfortunately—" Dr. Patar cleared her throat. "—there is only cognitive or talk therapy and perhaps hypnosis."

"There's nothing you can prescribe?" Nick's mother asked. His dad sat back, folding his arms.

"We can try a serotonin inhibitor. That drug is mainly used for depression."

"He's certainly been depressed!" Nick's dad huffed.

"Is it okay for me to go back to school?" Nick asked, and his parents turned to study him.

"Of course!"

Nick beamed.

"I'll check with the cardiologist," Dr. Patar said. "I think school would be good for you."

His parents and Dr. Patar talked about DID while Nick zoned out, a feeling of heaviness blanketed him. His mood lifted when he remembered Emily would return to help with his homework tonight. He glanced at the clock before catching his mom's eye, and they shared a small smile.

"I'd like to put together a treatment plan and see

Nick weekly."

They agreed and quickly left. Neither of Nick's parents said much.

****

"You look better today," Emily said as she unzipped her backpack and withdrew the paper he had written with Cat on Saumur.

"Every day, I feel more like myself again." He placed the paper face down on his desk. Cat's presence was still wedged between them. The elephant in the room.

"I know it's not the Christian thing to say," Emily said, looking at the paper, "but I'm glad she's gone." She didn't need to elaborate on who she referred to. They both knew.

Nick steered the conversation to school. "Okay, what have we learned about the Korean War so far?"

Emily drew out her notebook and found the page, reading her notes to him. "Conflict between North and South Korea." Nick leaned closer so he could smell the flowery shampoo Emily used. He wanted to put his arm around her and kiss her rather than talk about Korea.

Nick closed his eyes as she talked, nodding at the key points, but he let his arms cross over his chest.

"Communist North Korea invaded South Korea in 1950," Emily continued talking, whereas Nick's mind jumped to images of war. "America occupied non-communist South Korea."

Nick felt suddenly tired and felt his head tilt toward Emily's shoulder. He rested on her as she continued to talk. She didn't push him away, and he felt heavy with sleep as Emily continued talking.

"Nick?"

He felt her hand on his arm, and he jerked upright.

"Sorry."

"I think you need a nap."

His eyes snapped open as she helped him to the bed before tiptoeing out of the room.

He wished she could stay, sleep with his head next to hers, and he was sure the dreams wouldn't bother him as long as she was near.

Chapter 19

"You there! Soldier! Why are you limping?"
Sawbones frowned at me, motioning toward my leg with
the bloody tool of his trade—a saw. I cringed at the
thought of the teeth biting into my leg, metal incisors
sinking deeper and deeper into my flesh.

Even though I had assisted with the surgeries, they
could hardly be considered surgeries: mutilations—a
better descriptor. I didn't know the doctor's Christian
name—Sawbones would have to do.

"Stiff leg," I mumbled.

"Have you been wounded?" Sawbones asked.

Should I lie to the doctor to save my leg? "Just an
old injury from when my mule kicked me."

The spot where I'd been shot was festering with
yellowish pus, and a snake of vile purple was slowly
inching up my left leg. I had tried to dislodge the ball
with a knife, but with a surface injury, the metal ball lay
just out of reach of my probing knife. My futile attempts
brought tears to my eyes. The light was poor, and my
efforts made the injury worse.

I had helped the surgeon cut off the legs and arms
of others with the same ailment. No, I wanted to keep
my leg despite the unbearable pain. I must keep my leg,
or my family would starve—I was a farmer, after all. A
farmer with one leg wouldn't be of use to anyone. But
how had they fared the last two years with me being

gone? Emeline with the young'uns? Sophia was six, Anne was only four when the war started, and I was called to serve. Wars were a senseless waste; the once superior Southerners, sure of their entitlement, were hopelessly losing. My farm straddled the North and South. I could have gone either way—I picked the North.

The North was winning, but morale was low, and we lost soldiers daily. Men were sneaking away to their homes and loved ones. I was torn—to leave or to stay— food in short supply and my boots gaping at the toe. There were no footwear replacements among the living, but I could steal from the dead. They wouldn't mind— they had escaped the misery of this terrible war, making their peace with the All Mighty, enjoying their just rewards from this strife-filled life.

Honor and duty were one thing, a hungry belly and cold feet, another.

My last letter from home had been months ago, crumpled and stained as if it had been carried in a knapsack for many weeks, which it most certainly had. How had my family survived the two long years I had been away fighting? Emeline only talked about teaching the little ones to read and tending her vegetable garden, nothing of the acres of corn, sorghum, and tobacco. Who was tending to the crops while I was away? Had the grounds gone fallow waiting for my return?

What of the plowing? I had ridden the donkey to war, but sadly the donkey had been requisitioned. I would have to pull the plow myself, with Emeline guiding me along the way. Could I plow with one good leg? I didn't think so.

No, sir, the leg must stay as long as I could bear the pain. I gritted my teeth together and prayed nightly, "Dear Heavenly Father, save me from the horrible purple snake in my leg."

Now I watched the cat, Stormy, meticulously clean her paws, her pink tongue flicking in and out. She dined on the scores of mice in the tents. It was her job to keep the mice at bay. I noticed she sat by the dying men, sensing somehow their pending deaths. She was known as the cat of death. Although she came to me, I didn't feel death at my doorstep. There was a distinction between her interest in me and her uncanny ability to sense death in others. Some of the men beckoned her closer. They had a knowing. Others didn't want her by their side.

"Bad omen," one had said when Stormy came to his blood-stained cot and waited. It wasn't long before I saw one of the orderlies remove the now deceased soldier and replace him with another.

"Shoo!" A man waved his remaining arm as Stormy ventured forward. "Stay away from me!" he cried. "I don't want to die."

I was sure the soldier would die by the way Stormy watched him while flicking her tail. The soldier would go honorably and not end it the cowardly way. With that end, he'd be welcomed into the Heavenly Kingdom, whole and well.

Chapter 20

Thanksgiving arrived with snow flurries, but that wasn't unusual for Michigan. November was often cold and icy.

Nick went downstairs to see if he could help. "Did you wring that fowl's neck?" Nick asked his father.

His mother gave him a concentrated stare. "I bought it at the grocery store," she replied, her eyes darting around the room as if she didn't believe what he had just said and thought of a plausible explanation.

Nick shrugged and felt a coldness seep into his being. He had said the wrong thing again.

"We're ready to eat," his mother said.

Nick greeted his grandmother before washing his hands.

Nick's father said a blessing, and they began passing around the food.

Nick loved Thanksgiving with the stuffed bird and his stuffed stomach afterward.

Grandma said, "I don't care where it came from. This is one fine meal!"

Nick's mother gave Grandma a pained smile and continued studying Nick.

On some level, Nick knew there was a disconnect between what he was remembering and what was happening now. He was in the present but remembering the past.

Nick's mom leaned forward and whispered, "Are you still hearing voices in your head?"

Not voices, but whole scenes complete with sounds, smells, and tastes. Hardly just voices in his head.

"Voices?" Grandma asked. "I hear them all the time! Especially when I don't have my hearing aid in."

God bless Grandma for her insights and comments. Nick smiled at her as she helped herself to more cranberry sauce.

"Apparently"—Nick put a napkin in his lap—"I have voices speaking to me from bonking my head repeatedly."

"Well, of course!" Grandma said. "All those tackles on the football field might have jarred something loose." She made a face. "I don't have that excuse. I've never played football or been tackled." She giggled. "Though, one time, your grandfather—"

"Mother!"

Nick grinned, wishing his mother hadn't stopped Grandma. He could tell Grandma was winding up to tell a whopper of a story. He'd have to remember to ask her about it when his mother wasn't around to interrupt.

Chapter 21

On Wednesday, Nick's first day back to school, his mother drove him, just like his first day of elementary school. They parked near the school entrance. Nick got out slowly and surveyed the building. He had been in the hospital or convalescing at home for six weeks. The rectangular school with similarly shaped windows appeared to be the same as before. The only difference was a carpet of snow on the lawn and roof.

Nick's mother got out and insisted on carrying his backpack. "This weighs a ton, Nick. I'm not sure you should be lugging this around," his mother said, lifting the bag and judging its poundage.

"I won't. Most of those books go in my locker."

"Good." They went into the office, where the principal greeted them.

"Welcome back," Principal Colbert said, shaking his hand.

The counselor, Mr. Robinson, came into the office carrying a stack of papers. "Nick! Glad you're back. Just stop by my office if you need anything—and I mean anything."

Nick dipped his chin to acknowledge the counselor's comments.

When they finished in the office and his mother left, he stepped into the crush of student bodies to reach his locker.

"Nick!" he heard his name chorused down the hall. "Nick!" Followed by "Hey! Nick!" He was happy to be back in the thick of things.

Emily joined him, staying by his side, gluing their two bodies into one as they navigated the packed junior locker section where he stowed his books.

He was exhausted from explaining what had happened and why he had missed so much school.

His day began in World History with Coach Sullivan, and he was glad.

Coach clapped Nick on the back in the way of a greeting. "Good to have you back in class."

Even Bryan nodded, acknowledging his presence. Could bully Bryan be happy to see his nemesis? His nemesis who was back with Emily—sort of.

Returning to school after being gone for over a month was strange. Everyone was friendly to him. Nick noticed their forced smiles and cheerful hellos as he walked through the hallways to class and his locker. They treated him like a new student even though he had attended school with most of them since they moved to Laketon many years ago.

He managed to get through three classes before putting his head on the desk.

"Are you okay, Nick?" his calculus teacher asked, her brows knit together, questioning.

He sat up and rubbed his face. "Sorry."

"No worries, this is your first day back."

He snuck a look at his phone and was glad for the abbreviated schedule he, his mother, the principal, and the counselor worked out.

Emily walked him to the front of the school when it was time to leave.

"See you later?" He jutted his chin out.

"Do you want to see me?" Emily asked.

"Yes!" He felt his mouth crack into a big grin.

She smiled and wiggled her fingers at him.

Just then, his mother pulled up to the curb. He never thought he'd be glad to see her blue Subaru, but as soon as she stopped, he managed to open the door with difficulty. The door weighed a ton! He plopped inside, fumbling with his seat belt before his mother leaned over to help him clasp it.

"How was it?" she asked.

"I feel like I could sleep for a week."

"Give it time," his mother said, her hands firmly on the wheel in the ten and two position, but the car wasn't moving.

"But I'm so far behind!" His hands flopped down by his knees. "How am I supposed to do all that missed work?"

"Give it time."

Like eating an elephant—one bite at a time.

****

Nick's first week back at school was uneventful until Emily met him by his locker and looked at him like she had a question.

"Would...would you take me to the Christmas dance?" she asked.

Did that...did that mean...they were officially or unofficially back together?

"Uh, sure!"

"Will you ask your parents if you can take me? Or me take you?" she pleaded.

He couldn't drive yet, so Em would have to take the wheel.

"I'll talk to them tonight."

Later, at dinner, he said, "I want to go to the Christmas dance."

"A dance?" His father raised a brow. "Are you up to that?"

When Nick thought about it, it wasn't a strenuous activity. Students would stand around and drink punch. The girls would admire their friends' dresses while the guys stood awkwardly in their best slacks and dress coats, longing for their jeans and sweatshirts. Everyone would be on their best behavior until maybe someone spiked the punch when the chaperone wasn't looking. If they danced, it would be to a slow song. Nothing was taxing about going to a dance.

"It's probably easier than going to class," Nick admitted.

"I guess," his mother said hesitantly.

He took her words as a yes. "Emily will be happy."

"Emily?" His father raised both brows.

"Are you back together again?" his mother asked.

"Sort of."

His parents remained quiet and waited for him to continue.

"We're taking it slow," Nick said, letting out a noisy breath.

"Slow is good." His father nodded.

"I guess the dance might be okay," his mother said. "Provided you're home early."

Nick tired quickly, so that shouldn't be a problem.

He went upstairs to text Emily and found a message waiting for him. The text message was short. —*Miss me?*—

Nick frowned at his telephone. The number was

unfamiliar. He typed: —*Who is this?*—

Neon green highlighted the words, and his stomach felt seasick and woozy.

—*Who do you think?*— Came the reply.

—*IDK.*—

—*Who do you want it to be?*—

Was the message from Cat? He hoped not. Or did he? The area code was 541, not the usual 616 for Laketon. He searched for 541. Damn, it was from Oregon. Had Cat gotten a new number?

He had pushed all thoughts of Cat away. She wasn't good for him. Sure, he lusted after her perfect dancer body but constantly felt like he was standing in the middle of a teeter-totter and, at any minute, would fall.

Also, when he was with her, he questioned himself constantly. With Emily, it was easy to fall back into their comfortable routine.

He texted Emily he could attend the dance before turning off the phone, placing it face down, and beginning his homework. All thoughts of the cryptic messages and who sent them were pushed away by sheer willpower. They may hover near his consciousness until he locked them away, not wanting to think about Cat returning to Laketon. She was the only person he could think of who would text him like that.

Oh, God, he hoped she wouldn't return when his life was starting to resemble "normal."

Chapter 22

Nick dressed for the dance, humming while slicking his hair back and adjusting his tie. He was taking Emily to the Christmas dance, or rather, she was taking him. Nick didn't care who drove. He was happy to get out of the house and away from watching television with his parents.

He thought of little else, except feeling a stab of fear at the taunting text messages from the Oregon area code. He forced his thoughts away from the chill of seeing Cat again and instead imagined burying his nose in Em's hair and being alone with her.

Downstairs he heard the doorbell chime. Emily! He ran down the steps but stopped as a twinge hit his knee. Dang, what was that? He moved his leg around and gingerly massaged his knee before walking sedately the rest of the way as his mom opened the door.

"You look beautiful!" Nick's mother said when she saw Emily's dress and updo.

Nick seconded his mother's appraisal, nodding with a silly grin.

"Thank you." She twirled around for further inspection. "Nick?"

Suddenly he was at a loss for words, nodding his head before handing her the wrist corsage he bought, and she pinned a boutonniere to his lapel.

A fleeting image ran through his head of a little

girl twirling around in an old-fashioned dress, saying, "See, Daddy, my new dress!" He knew the girl's name was Sophia.

Nick shook away the vision.

"Pictures!" Nick's mother said, snapping away as they stood, arms around each other.

"Take good care of our boy tonight," his father said. "And have fun!"

Nick's mother said, "Remember, home early."

Nick rolled his eyes.

"Don't think we didn't see that," his mother said with a smile.

"I'll get him home early," Emily promised. She wore a short jacket over her shimmering red dress, and Nick, his only pair of dress pants and jacket that halfway fit. He had put on some of the weight he had lost being sick, although he still felt like the scarecrow from the *Wizard of Oz*, flapping around in his clothes, the stuffing falling out.

"You look great," he said to Emily after they had exited the house and stood on the front porch, just the two of them. He squeezed her fingers in his.

"Thank you." The sparkle in her eyes outshone her dress. She was excited to be going to the dance with him.

He leaned toward her, and she did the same, and they sealed the compliment with a kiss before he took her arm and guided Emily to her car.

They drove to the Hearthstone to meet Gary and Tiffany. The place was packed, and everyone attending the dance had reservations. They were seated by a table of six where Bryan sat within earshot. He cast dagger eyes at Emily.

Emily greeted everyone at the nearby table. "You guys look amazing!" Everyone responded except Bryan, who looked away and drank his water.

Nick did the Christian thing and extended a "Merry Christmas" to him.

Bryan nodded at Nick's greeting but didn't return his acknowledgment.

Nick put on his most sincere smile, while inside, he muttered, "And shove it up your"—his smile grew bigger—"ass."

Chapter 23

After dinner, Emily drove them to the school gymnasium, aka "Christmas Wonderland." Nick flashed back to the last dance there—homecoming and the disastrous kiss with Cat culminating with Emily breaking up with him. He decided he didn't want to dwell on that night—tonight would be their new beginning. This dance would be far different than the last one. There was no Cat to wreak havoc.

"Wait until you see the decorations," Emily said. "We worked all afternoon getting everything in place."

Emily amazed him. Even after working on decorations, she still managed to look this good.

He wasn't particularly interested in what color the balloons were or the tinsel. He just liked spending time with Emily. It felt good to pick up where they left off—BC, Before Cat. That girl had turned his life upside down. He was returning to a somewhat routine and didn't feel the tightness in his chest from holding his breath, waiting for something else to knock him off track.

The school parking lot was already slushy and muddy from all the cars and feet stomping toward the gymnasium.

"Shall I drop you off at the door?" Emily asked.

"Nope, I'll walk you in. I'm not an invalid."

"I know, I know." She slowed the car, searching

his eyes. "I'm not suggesting you're not normal. It's good to have you back, but I don't want you to get sick."

"I already feel kind of conspicuous." Nick slumped in his seat. "The guy who lost the game, who got sidetracked by the goth girl, the guy in the hospital…"

"Let's not talk about any of that tonight." Em maneuvered into a parking spot. "I want us to have a good time."

"Me too," Nick agreed.

Nick unbuckled his seat belt and glanced out the window. What rotten luck. They parked next to Bryan's truck.

Before they left the car, Nick leaned over, inhaled Emily's fragrance, and kissed her. Their lips lingered, passionate, and when they pulled apart, Emily peered into his eyes. "My Nick is back!"

He was glad she thought that. He had a ways to go still.

They got out, held hands, and slowly headed toward the gym. Nick looked down at their entwined hands, Emily's swallowed by his, and realized it felt right.

Emily checked her coat at the entrance before entering the darkened gym. Music seeped out, muted by the crush of bodies. Silver and red streamers hung from the ceiling, twirling from the moving air inside the room. Balloons formed an arch over the doors, and a DJ was near the table for refreshments. The punch and cookies were guarded by their English teacher, Mrs. Mattley, who nodded and smiled as they came in.

"Would you like punch?" Nick asked.

"No." Before scanning the room, Emily glanced at

the refreshments, looking for her friends.

Nick shrugged okay as he helped himself to the punch. He took a sip and screwed up his face—someone had already spiked it. The vodka warmed him and made the room grow brighter. He gulped the rest down and tossed the cup into the trash.

Boldly, he took Emily's hand.

Veronica walked by with her date and nodded to them. Nick didn't recognize the guy. Perhaps he went to a private school in one of the neighboring towns. "Heard from Cat?" she asked.

Nick felt Emily stiffen.

"No, why?" His thoughts immediately went back to the messages from the unknown number.

"I think she texted me," Veronica said, dismissively waving her hand.

"Hmm." Nick kept his face a neutral expression and didn't react.

Emily crossed her arms. "I hope she's not coming back!"

Several couples were dancing to a slow song.

Nick moved his chin toward the dance floor and tugged lightly on her arm.

"Let's find a place to sit first," she said, taking his hand and guiding him toward the seating area.

Around the gym's perimeter were small tables accommodating four to six people. They spotted Gary and Tiffany.

"Come on!" Nick motioned for Em to follow.

The music moved up a notch, and talking was difficult. The attendees retorted by mouthing and shouting at each other. "This way!" Nick said as he pushed through people, finally able to reach Gary. He bumped his shoulder to say hi as Emily and Tiffany hugged. Gary looked over at Nick, and Nick nodded to Gary, unspoken guy communication for "let's get this done and over with so we can go out in the car and be with our girls."

Nick mouthed, "Punch?"

Emily pretended to punch him and then started laughing. Gary and Tiffany rolled their eyes.

"Dance?" Emily asked.

Nick thought it sounded like "dunce," which he probably had been earlier in the year, but he nodded, and they made their way to the dance floor.

They began dancing slowly, and it felt good for Nick to have his arms around Emily again. This was how it was supposed to be, with Emily leaning against him. They fit well together. Nick smelled the flower fragrance of her hair. He could have stayed this way forever until his left leg buckled. Nick clawed at the air, trying to find something to break his fall, almost taking Emily down. She screamed when he landed heavily on his hip. He had no warning!

"Help!" she yelled.

Damn, the floor was hard. Nick rubbed at the impact spot before getting on his hands and knees and starting to rise, unable to quite push himself upright. He felt as rubbery as pasta. His knee was unstable and felt like it would buckle again. He put an arm around Emily to keep him upright.

The music stopped, and people rushed forward.

"Are you okay?" Emily gasped.

"Am I bleeding?"

"No," she said, leaning closer to see his leg. "I don't see any blood."

"My leg is bleeding. I feel it."

"I'm so sorry, Nick!" Emily said, her face hovering close to his, lips by his ear. "Maybe this wasn't such a good idea."

Gary helped steady him. "What happened?"

"My leg." Nick rubbed at it, feeling the reassuring limb, although he thought he felt blood seeping through his pants. "I think I need to get home to Emeline."

Gary frowned. "Em's right here."

Nick stared at Emily blankly, his mind refusing to focus. He remembered someone else named Em, but he couldn't figure out who.

"Should I take you home?" Gary asked.

I needed to rest and get out of the cart. The straw was covered in blood, and I felt light-headed.

"Yes, I need to go home to my girls." Nick gasped.

Gary frowned as if he didn't hear correctly.

Emily grasped at his arm. "Are you okay that I have to stay to clean up?"

Nick nodded. "I'll call you tomorrow."

Emily turned to Gary and said, "Thank you."

"I think someone spiked the punch." Nick swallowed weakly. His head felt like it might float away.

Gary raised his brows but didn't respond. They didn't even talk much on the way home. Nick rubbed at his sore hip. Once there, Gary helped him into the house.

"You're home early," his mother called from the kitchen, and when she emerged, she saw Nick propped up against Gary. "What happened?"

"He fell," Gary said as if that explained it all.

"Nick?"

"Yeah." Nick nodded. "I did. Maybe you were right. It was too soon."

"Are you hurt? Do we need to take you to the hospital?" His mom's voice started to panic.

No hospital. "I think maybe dancing wasn't in the cards tonight." He absently rubbed at his leg, hoping the blood had stopped.

"What happened to taking it easy?" His mother calmed down, gently taking his arm, pulling him closer to the sofa, and making him sit.

"You going to be okay?" Gary asked, edging toward the door. "I should get back to Tif and the dance."

Nick's mother turned to Gary. "Thank you, Gary, for being such a good friend."

"Yeah," Nick said. "Thanks, man." And gave Gary a raised hand.

"We hope to see you and your family during the holidays," Nick's mother said.

"Me too," Gary said before leaving.

Nick heard the car start, the gravel crunching as Gary left their drive.

Nick's mother felt his forehead. "You don't feel warm."

I wouldn't be warm, would I? It was cold in Kentucky. I felt chilled to the bone.

"I'm not ailing if that's what you mean."

"Ailing?" His mom frowned slightly. "That's an interesting word." But before she could say more, the signal sounded on the oven. "I'll be right back," she said.

His telephone vibrated in his pocket, and he fished it out. —*We're coming back.*—

Oh, damn, another cryptic message from the 541 area code. It had to be Cat. She was the only person he knew in Oregon. She had been messaging Veronica too.

Another ping. This time it was a familiar number.

—How are you? Do you need me to come over after we clean up?—

Emily.

He texted back.

—No. Just tired.—

—I'll stop by tomorrow.—

—K—

Nick was about to shove his phone into his pocket when *—Have you missed me?—* Pinged. *Anonymous, though most certainly Cat.*

No, he didn't miss her. He did earlier, but when she didn't respond to his texts, he wrote her off. She was the reason for the reincarnation/dissociative personality disorder.

"I'm turning in," Nick said when his mother returned and sat on the couch next to him, realizing he hadn't seen his father. "Where's Dad?"

"Sick parishioner."

Nick got to his feet, testing his weight on his left leg, and a shooting pain went through his thigh. He winced and hopped one-legged to the stairs. "Night."

"Nick! Can't you put any weight on that leg?"

He shook his head.

"I think we'd better take you into urgent care and have that x-rayed."

Nick yawned. "How about in the morning."

His mother peered at him. "You might have pulled something." She jumped up from the couch and put a hand on his shoulder. "Do you need my help?"

"I'll need to learn to do things myself." He grabbed the rails on either side and hoisted himself up the steps.

"You must take things slow and easy for a bit still."

If things were going to get back to normal, he needed to think about what he said before he spoke.

Carefully he went up the steps, leaning heavily on the railing for support, keeping his weight mainly on his right leg. If Cat returned, he'd have to face his former life again, and he didn't want to do that.

Chapter 24

My dearest Emeline:

I'm glad you won't starve. You were always such a resourceful woman, and I have always loved you for your ways.

My job is to assist in surgeries, and when not helping the sawbones, I use a tonic to treat wounds. I have seen some terrible mortifications of the flesh—men who have lost fingers, eyesight, and hands from a misfired canon. The tonic looks like blood but keeps infections and festering sores away.

I've named my cat Stormy for the rain I rescued her from. She's tiny but has assisted me by licking some of the soldiers' wounds and improving them. I wouldn't have believed a cat could do such a thing. The men who are saved love Stormy, but those on the brink of death shy away from her. I'm not sure how she knows such an omen, but she waits by the cots of some men, and in the morning, they have left their mortal bodies.

We are running short on drugs to ease the pain. Some men have used what little we have left to end their own lives rather than live as a cripple. Several have taken opium or morphine and ended their suffering. The priest said their souls are doomed to eternal Hell, but living can be hell too. Please excuse my frank language. I'm tired of war.

Your ever-loving husband, Jonathan

****

Stormy, no Minnie, jumped on his bed and jiggled Nick. His leg still hurt, but he didn't feel like getting out of bed. What had he done to it besides dancing?

His mother came into his bedroom. "Aren't you going to get up?"

"Maybe," Nick said. "My knee still hurts."

"I think I should take you to get an x-ray. Maybe you tore or bruised something?"

Nick struggled to wakefulness, feeling under the covers for blood-covered straw, only finding sheets warm from his body. Still, his body felt itchy and out-of-sorts, and his knee felt hot to the touch.

She felt his forehead, her mouth in a line. "How are you feeling?"

"Do I feel warm?"

"I can't tell." She tried kissing his forehead. "I don't think so," she said.

The festering in his leg stopped.

Minnie leaped where she had been and landed on his leg. "Oh! My leg!" Nick gasped, feeling beads of sweat on his brow.

"You might have pulled something," Mom said.

He couldn't think what he had done to pull anything. He hadn't played football in weeks. Should he tell his mother he had lost his leg in the war? Would she understand? "Yeah, something like that," he mumbled.

His mother patted his shoulder, pivoted on her heels, and said, "I'm going to call Dr. Garson and see if he can recommend someone to see you for your knee pain."

Nick slumped back into the pillows, and Minnie

climbed next to his head. She surveyed the bed and alternated licking her paws and cleaning her whiskers. Minnie had remained on his bed, by his side, but a sentry of what? She was a soothing presence as he waited for the bleeding to stop.

Nick shook himself mentally. He needed to get hold of his thoughts. When he glanced down at his leg, it was whole. He blinked and looked again. He could have sworn... He could have sworn it was gone. It felt cut off, but there was a complete whole leg, no blood-crusted stump. Sure, it hurt, but it was all there.

Oh God, what had Cat started in him? A chain of events that hadn't stopped even when she was gone. Could Dr. Sims help? Or even Dr. Patar? He put his money on Dr. Sims. Could she make sense of this past-life intrusion on his current being?

From far away, he heard the doorbell chime. He waited, holding his breath. Would his mother answer the door, or had she gone to church? The bell sounded again, echoing through the empty house.

He climbed out of bed, gingerly putting weight on his left leg, then angrily stomping down. His leg was whole! He felt his heel slam into the floor, sending a pain shooting up the back of his leg. Damn, that hurt. He parted the blinds and saw Emily walking back to her car. He had missed her. Damn! He scrubbed at his face. He needed to get a grip. Did he really pull or sprain something in his knee or was it all in his head? He reached down to feel his knee. It hurt to the touch. Yes, the pain felt real.

Chapter 25

Nick and his mother drove to Speedy Stop Medical Care for his leg. Nick wobbled in using his walker, keeping most of his weight on his right leg. His mother explained what had happened, filled out the insurance forms, and they waited.

Nick was surprised at the number of people here for a Sunday afternoon.

Finally, they were called. Nick's leg was x-rayed, and now they waited in an exam room where a doctor met them.

"Hi, I'm Dr. Leavy," she said, extending her hand to Nick. "What seems to be the problem?"

"My knee gave out at the dance last night."

"Hmm. Were you doing the renegade or the box?" she asked, giving a little snort.

Nick raised his brows at his mother and shrugged. "Don't know those dances," he said. "We were slow dancing."

"Oh." She put Nick's x-ray on the screen. "I don't see a fracture of any kind. You may have torn or injured soft tissues. It doesn't show up on an x-ray." She paused and gauged their expressions before turning back to the screen.

"Can you check to see if something is torn?" Nick's mother asked. "He has played football since he was little."

Dr. Leavy nodded. "Football can damage the ACL. I'll order an MRI scan to tell us more than an x-ray." She felt down his leg and probed at his knee, which was now swollen.

Nick winced and didn't want to cry out like a sissy, but dang, that hurt.

"If I had to guess by your expression of pain, I think you may have damaged or torn a ligament. Can you put any weight on it?"

Nick shook his head. "No."

"If you don't mind waiting a little longer, we can do an MRI and know for sure."

Nick and his mother went back to the waiting area, where Nick scrolled through his messages, mainly from people asking how he was. He answered some until he saw another message from the Oregon number.

—*Should be back before Christmas.*—

Nick scrunched up his mouth and rolled his eyes. Just great. What else could go wrong?

Soon they went to a room with a large machine that scanned Nick's leg. He was happy to be out of that machine which vibrated with whirling sounds and made him think he was in a submarine.

Yup, he had a torn ligament. This day was turning out to be quite crappy. First, Cat was returning, and he might have surgery to fix his leg.

"We may be able to repair it arthroscopically," Dr. Leavy said.

Anything to get him back on his two feet again!

After spending almost five hours there, Nick decided Speedy Care wasn't very speedy. But he knew what was the matter with his knee.

Chapter 26

Nick and his father had an appointment with an orthopedic surgeon for his ACL tear.

A woman doctor—Dr. Hollingsworth—smiled at Nick and his father and explained what she would do during surgery. "It appears you have torn your anterior cruciate ligament. Quite common for some athletes."

Nick nodded, but his eyes darted around her office, taking in her medical diplomas and a knee diagram. The knee looked complicated. Besides the anterior cruciate ligament, there was a patella, tibia, and lateral collateral ligament—each represented in a different color. Her office reminded him of Dr. Garson's, except Dr. Garson had pictures and models of a heart, not a knee.

She paused as if waiting for questions, but when neither Nick nor his father responded, she continued, "I'll use a small hole next to your knee to do the reconstruction. I'll first look around and ensure there isn't more damage than what the images show."

"How do you see inside?" Nick asked, mystified at how she could do that.

"A tiny magnifying device." She showed Nick something the size of a skinny pencil.

"That?" he asked.

"Yup."

She showed Nick and his father a plastic model with rubber band "x's" representing the ligaments inside his knee. She would use one of his hamstring muscles to graft to his knee.

"Will he be able to play football again?" Nick's dad asked.

"Should be. Many sports figures have had this surgery done." She ticked a few names off on her fingers. "MM Youngblood, Bubba Williams, Alec Rivers."

Nick's dad nodded and rubbed his chin like he knew those names.

"The recovery isn't very long, and you should be on your feet in no time. But—" She held up a hand. "—no, I repeat, no football this year!"

Football was over, so no worries.

While Nick waited for the surgery, he was to stay off his leg as much as possible. He had no school until after his surgery.

He texted Emily on the ride home.

—*Having surgery on Friday.*—

—*Oh, no!*—

—*Torn ACL.*—

—*Do you want me to get your schoolwork?*—

—*No.*— He included a smiley face.—*I mean, yes.*—

An excuse to see Emily. She'd fuss over him when she brought his books. Maybe he could entice her to lie on the bed and comfort him. He could rest his head on her chest. But he shook away the pleasant image. There was no way Emily would allow that if his parents were home.

—*Can I come over after school?*—

—*Sure.*—

****

Nick and his parents headed for the surgery center on Friday at six a.m. The snow pummeled the car, and his father's wipers beat double time to keep the windows clear. Nick yawned widely. Why did they have to schedule him for nine o'clock in the morning? The roads were slippery, and they passed several trucks spreading sand over the icy sections.

Once there, the nurses hooked Nick to a bag of fluids, and he felt light-headed and sleepy. Dr. Hollingsworth had told him they'd make him groggy before making him sleep. A nurse came in and painted his left leg red and then shaved it.

Nick yawned and managed a lopsided grin. "So this is what chicks go through?" he asked.

"Yup!" she replied. "You ready to go into the operating room?"

"I guess. Maybe you should shave the other one, so I match."

She chuckled and patted him on the shoulder before pushing the bed toward the door and into a hallway marked with "surgery center."

Later, Nick's vision ebbed and flowed, alternating between bright and dark. His parents' faces were gray blobs of mismatched features.

"I need Stormy," he croaked.

"Did he say it's stormy?" his father asked.

"I think so."

Stormy wouldn't leave my side. The red-hot pain had reached almost to my groin.

"Git." I waved my arm feebly at the cat, recalling the other men's superstitions of pending death. She didn't move.

"Leave me!" Still, she stayed, resettling on my

chest.

"I can't get my breath!" I croaked.

"That leg must come off," the surgeon said, wiping his hands on his blood-soaked apron. Sawbones.

"No!" I cried. "How will I tend my farm?"

"Do you want to end up like those other men?" The surgeon waved his arm toward the distant field. I blinked at the mountain of dead bodies, the flies thick as tar. I turned away and wrinkled my nose at the stench. There were so many none of them had received a Christian burial.

"No, please! Please, don't take my leg!"

I was glad when my mouth was pried open, and whiskey blazed down my gullet.

"Now give him something to bite on."

I felt the metal bullet wedged between my teeth and the command, "Bite down."

They grasped me by the arms and legs before the saw ripped into my flesh, pain like nothing I had ever felt before—thunder and lightning, fire and hail, blistering my skin, my soul. When the saw reached the bone, I gave one last hoarse scream before succumbing to the heavenly black bliss.

When I awoke, I was in a straitjacket of agony.

"Give me something. I'm dying."

"You'll live. Give him some opium," a nearby voice ordered.

"None to be had."

"I want to die!"

And indeed I wanted to. The others had overdosed on opium or just went outside and stuck their side iron to their temples and pulled the trigger. Suicide. Could I damn myself to eternal Hell? As the pain cinched another notch in my leg, I wanted to. Oh, yes, I wanted to end it all!

"My son. I bless you, my son." A death-like figure dressed in black prayed over me.

"I have sinned," I moaned to the priest, or was he the devil? "Father. Pray for me!"

"Nick? Nick! It's Dad!"

My father, who art in heaven... I was sure I was dead.

Chapter 27

"Nick?"

Who in the tarnation was Nick? "No, don't do it!" He jerked away from the bonds holding him.

"Nick? It's your mother. You're in the hospital. You've just come out of reconstructive surgery for your knee ligament."

The bloody hospital tent? A wretched place that took men's souls, leaving their wasted bodies.

"I don't want to die."

"You're not going to die," a woman said, her voice soothing like the soft patter of rain on the roof.

"My leg." His arms were tethered by his side. He longed to feel down his leg, but he felt numb. His leg was gone. He was sure of it.

"You tore your ACL and had surgery." The voice was like a lifeline. His mother, he thought. But did he still have his leg? "When the antibiotics are finished, we can go home."

"What's an anti…" his tongue, a fat sausage, filled his mouth and made speech difficult. What was that strange word? Something the Southerners dreamed up?

"Medicine for infections," she said.

"I want whiskey."

"Whiskey?"

He felt a cool hand on his forehead.

"Sawbones took my leg."

"Hush, you need to rest."

He shrugged away from the hand. "Who will plow the fields?"

"He's feverish." Her voice turned sharp and anxious. "Nurse!"

He heard a ping from far away, then running feet.

****

The fever had left me when my leg was gone. Stormy stayed with me, but I didn't feel the grim reaper coming for me. No, Stormy was a great comfort, sitting by me—allowing me to talk and share my fears. She didn't comment or move, just listened, her ears twitching, eyes half-lidded.

"I'm scared, Stormy, and scared for the future. What of my farm? Who will tend it?"

I could no longer fight, so I decided to go home— home to Emeline and the girls. Maybe I'd bring the cat for their enjoyment.

"Would you like to go home with me? Back to Kentucky? The girls will like you, and you can catch mice all day long."

Stormy licked her paws, considering my offer.

"The corn crib is full of mice, and we have fat milk cows," I said.

She seemed agreeable.

I liked having someone to talk to, even if that someone was only a cat. I missed talking to my wife after the little ones were put to bed. Yes, I missed our conversations sorely.

****

Nick awoke slowly, taking in glimpses of the room first. It wasn't as he had expected. He thought he was in the hospital tent, but this room was white and sterile, nothing like what he remembered. First, his eyes fluttered open, taking in the squares on the ceiling, then to the metal sides of the bed and the television suspended overhead. Then his nose twitched—not the familiar smells of home, but of antiseptic cleaner with an undertone of something raw and fish-like. He licked his chapped lips. Water—he needed water.

He reached out his needle and tape-covered hand toward the enticing cup of water on the stand next to the bed.

Nick gingerly took the cup, guiding the straw toward his mouth. Almost there, his efforts clumsy and jerky, spilling most of the water down the front of his gown, managing finally to get the straw between his lips, sucking greedily, finishing the water in the cup. Now exhausted, he let the cup fall away before retreating into himself.

Stormy used her rough pink tongue to clean my thigh, working her way down to the stump.

My thoughts swam away in a clear, shallow pool of cool water—such a relief after the raging fire in my head.

****

"Would you like something to drink?" A voice came out of the darkness, saying magic words of hope.

He was thirsty and hungry.

Nick couldn't find his voice, instead waving his arm feebly.

"Nurse? I think he's coming around," an excited voice said. The voice was vaguely familiar. His mother. Grace. Grace Dupont was…he was Jo— No, Nicholas, Nick. She was his mother.

Chapter 28

Two weeks. That was how long I convalesced. Emeline's brother Garrett tended to me. When Garrett wasn't helping me, he began whittling on a piece of split rail stolen from a nearby farm. He shaped a hollow end for my stump and then turned the wood into the shape of a leg, with a sort-of foot at the bottom. It was a thing of beauty. I admired it, and so did Stormy. Others begged Garrett to make their arms and legs.

The mule-drawn cart loaded with supplies would take me to Fort Randolph, Tennessee. I'd have to find my way to Kentucky. I wished Garrett could have traveled with me, but Garrett was off fighting now.

What use would I be to Emeline? With my heart sinking with dread, I prepared to leave. There was no chariot to bring me to Kentucky except a cart with bags and boxes of produce. I couldn't find Stormy when it was time to leave.

When we were out of sight of the army, I heard a rustle and Stormy climbed out of my knapsack and surveyed the potatoes and onions with a twitch of her tail.

"How did you get in there?" I asked. "I searched for you." She rubbed her head against me and daintily stepped around the matted straw before stopping to lick her paws clean.

I dozed but was jerked from my fitful sleep by an

oozing of my bloody stump.

The driver came around the side of the cart. "Mother of God. The blood!"

"The movement opened the wound," I said, surveying the blood, suddenly feeling faint.

"We'll stop here for the night."

"Yes." My head swam, and I felt as light as a sparrow.

"Where did the cat come from?"

"A stowaway," I mumbled as I ripped off the bottom edge of my threadbare coat to tie around the stump the way I'd seen sawbones do, squelching the blood. It eased. But still, my head felt woozy and unfocused.

I leaned back against the rough sides of the cart and closed my eyes. I heard a rustle as Stormy climbed to the top of a potato sack to survey the scene. She wasn't the angel of death but rather the angel of hope for me. Then I floated away, as light as the onion peels on the persistent breeze.

I awoke sometime later from a nudge on my arm. The driver handed me a cup of beans. I offered a taste to Stormy, but she declined my offer. I ate the beans. The warmth filled my stomach, and I slumbered again.

Chapter 29

Dr. Hollingsworth tapped on Nick's door, and Nick squinted at the clock. It was 6:30 a.m. He didn't understand why they started so early.

The doctor stopped by Nick's bed and glanced down at the tablet in her hand.

"How are you this morning?" She moved the sheet aside and looked at Nick's knee before nodding and peering at Nick.

"I think I feel fine." He gave a rueful laugh. "It's early, and I'm still half asleep."

"Understandable. I want you up and walking," Dr. Hollingsworth said. "I've asked physical therapy to start working with you."

"It hurts."

"It shouldn't hurt that much. We went in arthroscopically and repaired the ligament."

"Didn't you cut off my leg?"

Dr. Hollingsworth laughed. "No. Does it feel that way?"

"I remember gangrene." Nick felt along his leg; sure enough, he still had a limb and frowned. He could have sworn they had cut it off. "Why am I here?"

"You had your ACL repaired," Dr. Hollingsworth said and tapped the side of the bed as she talked. "I don't think I've seen a case of gangrene before. We can up your dose of antibiotics."

"What are antibiotics?" Nick demanded.

Dr. Hollingsworth's brows shot upward, and she gave him a squinted stare.

"You've been on antibiotics before, Nick."

Nick shook his head stubbornly. "I've never heard of it before. Is it something new?"

"Yes, something new." Dr. Hollingsworth sighed. Nick could tell by her expression the doctor was humoring him. He didn't need humor. He needed to leave this place with the blood, antiseptic, and hospital smells.

"I'll send the physical therapist to help you out of bed."

And just how was he to walk with just one leg?

Nick dozed until he heard the door to his room open. It was a tiny swish, but he heard it all the same.

"Nicholas Dupont?"

"Jon..." He paused, shaking away the sluggish feeling. "Nick, please."

"Okay, Nick. Ready to get out of bed?" The therapist was a pretty girl with reddish-brown hair.

"I guess." He used his palms to scrub away the sleep from his eyes and then blinked. The blurriness was gone.

The therapist helped him sit and swing his legs over the side of the bed. "Slowly. You don't want to get dizzy."

He already felt his head swim. The therapist moved the walker closer, guiding his hands to grab the padded holders and ease into a standing position. Nick saw the name Julie on her badge.

"Julie," Nick grunted—his knees weren't cooperating, refusing to stay straight. "I don't... I can't…" Nick struggled.

"Good. Let's try that again."

Nick sat on the bed, catching his breath before the therapist pushed him upright for a second try at standing. He stood for an eternity, in reality, only a few seconds, before sitting back on the bed.

"You have to stand before you can walk. Just like a baby."

He was relearning the basics all over again.

"Third time is a charm," she said.

On this try, he managed to stay standing and take a few tentative steps, his left foot lagging.

"Is there any reason you're not putting weight on your left foot?" Julie asked.

Nick looked down at his leg. Before his very eyes, it morphed from whole to a stump and whole again. "It hurts."

"On a scale of one to ten, one being the worst pain, where are you?"

"Maybe a six." When he stepped forward, it didn't hurt, but if he closed his eyes, remembering the amputation, it hurt like hell.

She dipped her chin in acknowledgment. "We'll work more later."

****

After the physical therapy session, Nick dozed, hands brushing away the persistent flies swarming around his body, taking jabs at his bloody bandages. Vicious little creatures bent on tormenting him.

"Knock. Knock."

"Leave me alone! Damned flies!"

"Nick?"

Nick. The name caused him to stop swatting at the

black nuisances. People had taken to calling him Nick.

"What?"

"It's me, Emily. Can we see you?" she asked.

Emily. The name caused him to pause, searching his mind for the body that went with the face. The storage unit of his brain put a look with the name—a pretty girl with large eyes, made more prominent by her glasses perched on her upturned nose.

"Is…is it okay if we come in?"

"Sure." Nick sat up as Emily, Gary, and Tiffany entered the room.

"Hi, sickie," Emily said.

"What's new?" Nick asked—a lame question. They came to see him.

"We had a snow day!" Emily said as Tiffany squealed, "Snow day!"

School seemed like another century ago, and it was already snowing.

"Yup, we've got snow," Gary added with a low whistle.

Nick realized he hadn't looked out the window…had he even tried? He didn't think so.

"When can you get out of here?" Gary asked.

"Soon, I hope."

Nick yawned, and everyone agreed it would be best for him to rest. Before leaving, Tiffany leaned down, whispering in his ear. "Bryan's been bugging Em since you've been in here."

"Hey!" Gary held open the door. "What are you two whispering about?"

"Nothing." Tiffany stood up. "Just telling him how much we miss him." She winked and skipped out of the room.

Nick needed to leave the hospital. Stat—hospital slang for "in a hurry."

He didn't have long to think about a hospital exit plan when Emily slipped back into his room. Her rainbow-design sneakers announced her presence by squeaking on the tiled floor.

Nick held out his hand. "What's Bryan been doing to you since I've been gone?"

"Not much." But she didn't look at him when she said it.

"Em."

"Trying to kiss me. Putting his arm around me. Spreading rumors we're going out."

Nick grew hot. He'd like to smash Bryan's face.

Emily leaned over the bed, and he kissed her. "I've got to get out of here!" he whispered.

She kissed him again before leaving.

****

When Dr. Hollingsworth came in, Nick launched into the question of him going home. "I'm going stir-crazy here!"

She probed his knee. "I see you have healed physically."

"What did you just say?"

"You've been raving about losing your leg and having gangrene."

"The medicine gives me bad dreams," Nick said, hoping the doctor would buy his explanation.

Dr. Hollingsworth cleared her throat. "Sometimes anesthesia can do that."

"I've had strange dreams about war," Nick said. It was the truth.

"It's not for you to worry about. You need to get

well."

"I want to go home," Nick whined. "I want to get back to school."

"Let me review your latest lab reports."

"Tomorrow?" Nick asked.

"I'll see what I can do." Dr. Hollingsworth patted his shoulder. "I'd say you're on your way to recovery."

When Julie, the physical therapist, returned to work with him, Nick willingly sat up and swung his legs over the side.

"I want to go home. Nothing against you," he reassured the therapist. "I'm just sick of this place."

"I don't blame you." She smiled tightly, motioning with a clipboard for him to continue. "Okay, walk to the door for me."

He did, sans the walker.

"And back," she said.

He complied.

"You want to walk down the hall?"

"Sure. Past the nurses' station so they can vouch for me."

"Do you want to wear another gown to cover up?" she asked.

Nick gazed over his shoulder. There was a draft in the back from the loose gown. "Have I been flashing you?"

"Nothing I haven't seen before." She laughed. "Hazard of the job!"

"I guess," he said, his face flushing red while struggling into another gown Julie held. She fastened a belt around his waist to hold him if he stumbled. They proceeded out of his room and down the hall. He greeted the nurses, and one gave him a thumbs-up. Was this enough for Dr. Hollingsworth to let him go home?

"Tell Dr. Hollingsworth I was walking!" he said to them.

The thumbs-up nurse just smiled. "It'll cost you."

Nick laughed as they continued down the hallway.

After Nick's walking efforts, Dr. Hollingsworth said he could go home and even attend school after his antibiotics were finished. Half days for a week and then full-time. His parents came to take him home. Nick was packed and waiting.

"Eager?" his father asked.

Nick rolled his eyes. "That obvious?"

"Just a tad," his mother said with a laugh. Her smile told Nick she was as relieved as he was to get out of the hospital.

"Can you swing through the drive-thru for a burger and fries?" Nick asked, tired of the bland hospital food and obligatory pudding or gelatin cup. Even their so-called burgers lacked something. Spices? They didn't even taste like the drive-thru burgers full of fat and other unsavory things.

His father grinned. "I think I could eat one of those myself."

Nick's mother mocked annoyance and rolled her eyes. "You two are incorrigible!"

"Good to have our boy back," Nick's father said as they left the hospital parking lot and headed toward the drive-thru.

Chapter 30

Nick was home and lying in bed when his phone pinged, signaling he had a new text message. He hoped it was Emily. It wasn't.

—*Miss me?*— The 541 number again.

If he answered yes, would they reveal themselves?

—*We're on our way back.*—

He started to sweat.

—*Cat?*— Nick's hand shook, making it hard to type. He waited, his finger hovering over his phone, ready to… Didn't he know what? No response. He typed —*When?*—

With heart hammering, he watched the screen.

—*Soon.*—

He didn't have long to wonder about the mystery number or text messages. He started physical therapy three days after his surgery. When Nick went into the physical therapy facility, he felt at home. The gym they used was similar to the weight room, with bikes, barbells, rowing machines, and other equipment. He looked around for that pretty therapist, Julie. No such luck. He'd be working with Wayne, who was built like a linebacker. But Wayne seemed to know his stuff and made Nick work until he had sweat on his brow and was panting with exhaustion.

"Show me how you walk to the door," Wayne said.

Nick picked up his crutches and raised his brows in

a question.

"Can you do it without crutches?"

Nick nodded, pushed up from the chair, and slowly plodded toward the indicated door.

"Good!"

Wayne had Nick doing squats, riding the recumbent bike, and doing side leg lifts. When he finished, Nick was sweating. A more challenging routine than football!

"Now I want you walking the track," Wayne said, tapping his pencil on a clipboard he used to record Nick's progress.

Nick didn't see a track, only a yellow line around the room. That was the "track."

"I want you to start with two laps tomorrow, the next session, three, and then four. Got it?"

Nick nodded. After a week of working with Wayne, he was steady on his feet and ready to return to school. And he secretly thought he might be in better shape for football if he wanted to play again.

Chapter 31

"This here's where you get off," the cart driver said as he began to offload the onions and potatoes.

A saloon sign swung in the breeze, and I heard voices and the clink of glasses. A drink would wet my parched mouth, but I was close to home. Part of me wanted a drink and the other part, to see my family.

"Much obliged," I said.

"God speed." The cart driver tossed a potato and onion in my direction, and I stuffed them in my pockets for the missus. Then hoisting my knapsack, with Stormy peeking out, I swung away from the cart.

"So now, how do we get home?" I said to no one in particular and expected no answer, but I was surprised when I got one. *"You know what to do."*

"Who said that?" The voice surrounded me. I jerked my head to see if anyone else had heard it, but no one paid me much mind.

"It's me, Stormy."

Had the cat spoken in my head? Was I losing my grip on reality? A talking cat! How absurd!

"Just stand by the saloon, and someone will take pity on you, on us."

I swung the door to the saloon open and sniffed at the smells of beer, whiskey, and tobacco. My stomach involuntarily grumbled. Several horses were tied outside along with a dray, and a team of sturdy horses regarded me with little interest.

Presently the dray driver came out.

"Howdy." I nodded.

"Howdy, yourself, soldier. You from around here?" The driver checked his horses over and inspected the wheels of the cart. The back was loaded down with barrels and boxes.

"Nope, on my way home to Kentucky."

The driver perused me up and down. A one-legged man in a ragged uniform hardly looked threatening. "You lose yer leg in the conflict?"

"Yessir. I've been discharged."

"Hop on. I'll take you as far as Fort Thomas. That's where I stop. The least I can do for a soldier."

With some difficulty, I climbed into the back and found a comfortable spot. I was exhausted and cushioned my head against my knapsack and fell asleep.

Once in Fort Thomas, I would have to walk the last few miles on foot. I hadn't had time to write to Emeline and tell her I was coming home. What a homecoming it would be! I smiled to myself at the thought.

"Here!" the driver said. "Fort Thomas."

"Much obliged."

After many hours it seemed, I limped down the long drive to our farmhouse. It looked more weather beaten, but it was still standing, for which I was glad. Stormy rode with her head poking up, surveying her new home in Kentucky.

"Yoohoo!" I hollered, lest I scared them. "It's me, Jonathan!"

I waited, and presently, the door flew open. Emeline came running, skirts flailing around her ankles.

"Jonathan! Jonathan!"

She threw herself at me, knocking me off balance and pitching me to the ground.

"It is you!" she said, sitting up from the ground regarding me. "And..." Her eyes grew wide as she took in my appearance—my leg, splayed at an awkward angle.

"It's me, or most of me anyway." I shrugged. "The sawbones took my leg clean off from the gangrene."

"Praise the Lord in all his glory—you're home!" She hugged me.

"Best you not get too close," I warned. "I'm crawling with critters."

"Never no mind. We'll draw you a bath and get you a hot meal, and you'll be right fixed up!"

Stormy shook herself from the sack and began licking her paws from the tumble in the dirt.

"So this is the cat?" Emeline asked.

"Yup, I call her Stormy. Followed me here. She's a right smart cat, too! Thought the girls might like her. You know, as a pet?"

"Harrumph, no pets in the house." Emeline stood, dusted off her backside, and offered me a hand as I got to my feet and fastened the crutches under my arms. "She'll need to make do in the barn with the other cats."

"She's a good mouser, yes, ma'am."

I followed my wife to the back of the house with a large copper tub. Stormy trotted behind, her tail bristled and puffed out as she looked around. I was sure the unfamiliarity of the place made her cautious.

I sat and watched my wife dump pails of hot water

into the tub for my bath. I sat on an old stump and leaned against the side of the house, my eyes closing from the exhaustion and the trip here. Too, I was weak from the blood loss—as weak as a newborn colt, my mam used to say.

I awoke to a gentle shaking.

"Your bath's ready."

Emeline helped me shed my tattered, dirty, and vermin-covered clothing. She used a stick to pick up the pile and add them to the fire pit. I luxuriated in the tub. It had been... Lawd, I couldn't remember the last time I'd bathed. The water was blacker than the inside of my hat.

After Emeline's vegetable stew, we sat by the roaring fire in the kitchen.

"Sorry, we didn't have any meat for the stew—the Rebels stole most of the pigs and chickens." She put her hands together like she was praying.

"Better food than the army—meat or no meat. I'll have another bowl if there's any left after the young'uns get their fill."

To my surprise, there was more bread to sop up the gravy, too—a satisfying meal. After my bath, I wore my old coveralls and a frayed shirt. It was soft and felt good against my skin.

The girls, Sophia and Anne, nestled against my side, their heads on my lap. It was good to be home. Sophia held a book.

"Where'd you get that book?"

"Aunt Caroline brought it to us."

I took the book, turned it over, and looked at the cover. Alice in Wonderland. "What's it about?" I asked.

"Alice and all kinds of peculiar things. A talking cat called Cheshire."

"Did you see the cat I brought you?"

The girls straightened, eyes big. "A present?"

"Yes, she was a stowaway and took care of your old pa along the way."

"Can we see her?"

With some difficulty, I stood, hobbled over to the door, and called, "Stormy. Here. Kitty, Kitty."

"Is that her name? Stormy?"

"Yup! Found her in a storm."

After a short wait, Stormy appeared out of the deepening gloom and wound her way around my legs.

Sophia reached down and stroked her hair. "She's right soft."

"That she is," I said.

"Can I hold her?" Anne asked.

"If she'll let you."

Stormy purred contentedly against Anne's shoulder.

"She's pretty, Daddy."

I nodded. "She is."

"Girls!" Emeline said. "Put the cat in the barn and get ready for bed."

"But... Daddy... Can't the cat stay in the house?"

"No animals in the house! She's a barn cat," Emeline retorted.

I could see the disappointment on my daughters' faces. "How about we'll read that story when you're ready?"

Reluctantly, Anne put Stormy in the barn.

After the young'uns were asleep, I snuggled with Emeline in our feather bed, nestled my nose into the sweetness of her neck, and quickly fell asleep.

Chapter 32

Nick went back to school a week after his ACL surgery. He returned hiding a secret that could rip things apart for him and Emily. So he kept the knowledge that Cat would be returning to himself. No use upsetting everyone. What did soon even mean? Tomorrow? A week? The New Year?

He and Emily needed to be a cohesive front. Cat needed to see them together.

Christmas was just around the corner, and because of his hospital stay, his parents hadn't done any decorating.

On Saturday afternoon, Nick helped his father string holiday lights along the eaves of the house, a tedious endeavor of untangling the lines, replacing bulbs, and separating again. And searching for the extension cords.

"Your mother is always asking me to clean the garage, and it's times like these I wish I hadn't watched the last football game and done as she suggested," his father said, rubbing the back of his neck.

They opened and closed the various cabinets lining the unattached garage set back from the house, a dark and creepy place with only two small bulbs casting minimal light and cobwebs from corner to corner.

"Yup, she's always after me about my bedroom," Nick said.

"Your mother's a smart woman, and I'm glad I married her. She's my better half."

Nick laughed. "Mom loves you too." He wasn't sure of Emily's love. Maybe they were just too young to declare their love for each other.

"Yes, she certainly loves the disorganized men in her life."

Nick found the first extension cord in the drawer of a workbench, home to all sorts of gadgets and gizmos. Nick didn't know what half of them were for. "Found one."

"Me too," his father said, pulling out a cord wound as a figure eight from a cabinet. "I wonder why we don't store the cords in the same place?"

"We could do that when we clean the garage," Nick suggested.

"I guess there's no way around it," his father said as they went back to the front of the house, climbing up the ladder and plugging in the lights.

"Let there be light!" Nick said when they twinkled on. He remembered the "Christmas Vacation" movie with the house covered in lights—their house didn't resemble the movie house in the least.

"Hallelujah."

"I'll help you clean the garage if you like," Nick offered, feeling in the holiday spirit. Anything to get his mind off Cat—anything to get his mind off Emily.

"Thanks." His father climbed down and clasped him on the shoulder. "First, let's see if we can rustle some grub out of your mother."

"She'll want us to help put up the tree."

"Oh, Lord! Let's start on the garage. I hate putting up the tree."

"If you want," Nick said, stopping mid-step, preparing to turn back to the clutter and junk in the garage.

"No, we best get the tree out of the way, or there'll be no dinner for us tonight."

"You could make chili?" Nick suggested.

"That sounds good," his father said, rubbing his gloved hands together. "Brrr." He shivered. "But still, let's go get the blasted tree decorated."

Nick helped with the tree but sat down several times to rest his leg. There was no use pushing things and making his knee throb.

His father made his famous inferno, five-alarm chili, with a bite bringing tears to Nick's eyes as his mom poked at a jalapeño with her spoon. "I invited Grandma for chili, and she took a pass." She smiled. "Said it burned her tongue last time."

"It's not that hot..." Nick said, wrinkling his nose, though he secretly agreed somewhat with his grandmother.

"It's not called five-alarm for nothing," his father said.

"She's up for my pot roast if I make one, though. Do you think that's a hint?" Nick's mom asked.

"You make good pot roast, Mom," Nick said.

"So no one likes my chili?" his father asked in mock horror.

"No one said anything about not liking it." His mother stuck her tongue out at his father. "Just a little too spicy for *some* people."

"Are you one of them?"

"My lips are burned!" His mother scowled before wiping her mouth and taking a big mouthful of her iced water.

"Okay, okay, next time, I'll tone it down."

Chapter 33

I had been settled in for almost a week now. It was shore good to be home. I even took out my pistol and got a few rabbits for the stew.

As we were nestling down for the night, I saw a shadow against the wall as we settled into our feather bed. Emeline had warmed a brick for our feet, and it was toasty and cozy under the quilts. The shadow appeared to be some animal. Perhaps the girls had let Stormy in against their mother's wishes?

I hoped the cat wouldn't cause a problem. I ran my hand down Emeline's body, my fingers pausing on the swell of her breasts before tugging gently on the hem of her nightgown.

There was a slight bounce on the bed.

"What was that?" Emeline whispered.

I shifted onto my right side and nuzzled her neck. "What's what?"

"I felt the bed move," she said, pushing my hand away.

"I didn't feel anything," I lied.

Emeline sat up and moved her arms around the coverlet. "A cat!" She waved her arms. "Shoo!"

"The girls must have let it in," I grumbled.

"Well, put it out!"

I pushed her back against the pillows. "Later."

"I won't be able to sleep until it's gone."

"I wasn't thinking of sleeping just yet," I said.

She removed my hand from her thigh. She wasn't having anything to do with me until I put the cat out. I eased out of the warm bed into the room's chill and struggled into my crutches before shooing Stormy out the back door. Emeline was sleeping, snoring softly, when I returned. Darn, that Stormy.

Chapter 34

After putting up the tree and helping his parents decorate for Christmas, Nick got a text from Emily asking if he'd like to have Sunday brunch with her family after church. Nick had promised to help his father clean the garage, but he wanted to see Emily too.

A promise was a promise, though—but maybe, just maybe, his father could wait until they finished brunch.

Yes, his father could wait. Nick knew his father didn't want to tackle the garage, and any excuse to postpone it would be acceptable to him.

****

But now, Nick and his father stood in the open door and surveyed the dusty shelves, the boxes in the rafters, bins stacked on one another, and the clutter accumulated in each corner. The garage didn't seem as bad as before now that Nick's stomach was full of quiche, cinnamon rolls, fruit, and bacon.

"Why did I agree to this?" his father asked, rubbing his hands together. The garage wasn't heated. The cold winter air squeezed through the cracks around the windows and doors.

"Let's get it over with." His father let out a noisy sigh.

"Where do you want to start?" Nick asked, rubbing his gloved hands together.

"In my recliner watching a football game," his

father said. "I guess we better have a strategy. Start with the right and work our way around?"

They began with the tool bench. The hammers, screwdrivers, and pliers weren't in any organized manner. All were intermixed in one drawer. "I'll clean the drawers," Nick said.

He pulled out the clutter of tools, concentrated on putting all the like items together, and took frequent breaks when he felt tired.

There were four drawers, three relatively shallow and a deep drawer at the bottom. Nick opened the last one to find a box of old family pictures. Nick took out the photos and pulled a stool over to the bench.

"What do you have there?" his father asked, wiping his brow on the back of his work gloves.

"Pictures."

Together, they flipped through the primarily black-and-white photos. Some had faded to gray with only the ghost of an image available.

"These should be protected better than in a box in the garage." A water stain discolored the side of the cardboard.

Nick took out a picture of Grandma and Grandpa when they were younger.

"You look like your grandfather," his father said, peering over Nick's shoulder.

Nick did resemble his grandfather in some ways. Their chiseled noses and steady, piercing eyes were the same. He hoped he would never have cancer and end his life as Grandpa did.

Nick slipped the picture into his pocket as he continued riffling through the photos. Dupont relatives intermixed with Jenkins—Jenkins was his mother's side of the family.

His fingers touched something solid at the bottom of the box. A tin-type of a civil war soldier. "Who's that?" Nick asked.

"I don't know. Not one of my relatives." His father turned it over and squinted at the faded, smeared writing on the back. "Reb...or it could be Zeb...Jenkins. Aged 15...or maybe 16?"

Zeb hadn't been much older than Nick was currently.

His father handed back the metal picture. "Someone from your mother's side fought in the Civil War, I believe."

Nick studied the black-and-white image of the soldier in a lopsided cap, with stoic eyes and a grim set to his mouth. Nick imagined the war would harden a person, and this soldier looked pretty young. Only the eyes gave the impression he was older and had experienced the horrors of war. A pair of crutches were propped against the chair. Had he been wounded?

Coach Sullivan lectured the World History class about learning from the past. What could be gleaned about the Civil War? Slavery was wrong, and there were still repercussions today. And then, there was the personal knowledge about the war shared by Jonathan. Nick felt a prick of sadness at Jonathan's unfortunate circumstances.

"Those should be in the house in a more temperature-controlled environment," his father said.

Nick put the tin type into his pocket to question his mother later.

It was beginning to get dark when they finished. His father pulled off the work gloves and left them on the bench. Nick followed suit. Nick wiped his sweaty forehead with the back of his hand and followed his dad into the house. Brunch had been many hours ago, and he was starving.

"You two look like you've been rolling around in the dirt and spider webs," Nick's mother said, brushing away something from his father's arm.

The garage cleaning warriors, covered in dust and tired from their venture, were greeted by dinner smells as they entered. Nick's stomach grumbled in reply. Although the shelves were beginning to look more organized, they weren't done. Nick knew what each drawer contained.

"You should see the garage," Nick said, washing his hands before diving into the cookie jar. "Much better," he said, stuffing two cookies in his mouth.

"Easy, save your appetite." His mother laughed.

"We're starving."

"When aren't you?" His mother gave Nick a mock frown.

His father brushed away a smear of dirt as he walked past. "Shower time."

"I'm right after you!" Nick replied. He poured some milk and grabbed another cookie, eating it in two bites and washing it down with milk.

Nick drew out the picture for his mother. "Look what we found."

She frowned and reached for the photo. "Who's that?"

"Dad said it was one of your relatives."

"Could be." She held up the photo for a closer look. "We'll ask Grandma when she comes for dinner." His mother turned the picture over and squinted at the blurred writing on the back. She ran her finger over the raised design on the tin. "Amazing it has survived all this time! Look at the date."

Nick squinted at the 186...something date. The picture had survived over 150 years, probably lost in the jumble of various boxes and catchalls in someone's basement or attic until today. Now they were marveling at its age and imagining who the person was, not knowing their name or who they had been.

"I also found one of Grandma and Grandpa." Nick showed his mother another picture.

"Oh my, just look at my mother's curls!"

Nick had never seen his grandmother with dark curly hair. It had been straight and gray for as long as he could remember.

"Dad says I look like Grandpa."

Grace held out the photo and glanced from Nick to the image of his grandfather. "The eyes and nose?"

He saw her bite her lip as her eyes got bright with tears.

"I guess." Grandpa was lean and lanky in the picture. Nick had broader shoulders and a chest inherited from his father.

"I wish he were still here," Nick said.

His mother nodded before turning away and looking out the window at the still darkness.

Nick saw her wipe at her eyes in the reflection of the windowpane. He could tell by her tears she missed her father too.

Chapter 35

While Nick showered, his father picked up Grandma for dinner. While he dried off, Nick checked his telephone for messages.

—*I'll be home for New Year's.*— The 541 number again.

He knew the message had to be from Cat. Why couldn't she have left him alone and moved for good? Why come back and make a scramble of his life again?

"Do we know anyone from Oregon?" Nick asked his mother when she came upstairs with a load of towels in her arms.

"No," his mother said. "Not that I can remember."

Oh, how he wished they knew someone else besides Cat in Oregon.

"Why?" Her voice was muffled as she put the towels in the linen closet.

"I keep getting messages from a 541 number." Nick blew out a loud sigh.

She didn't respond when a buzzer sounded from the kitchen, and she hurried downstairs. Nick slumped on his bed before he heard, "Nick? Grandma's here!" his mother called.

He put on a shirt and said, "Coming."

When Nick came downstairs, his grandmother was sipping a small glass of wine and pretending to be interested in the football game his father had turned on.

"Nick!" she said excitedly. She set down the wine and started to get up.

"Sit." Nick waved his hands. "I'll come to you!" He reached down and kissed her cheek.

"You certainly look like your old self." She leaned back, appraising him. "No more operations? You had us worried."

"Nope, the doctor put me together again, and I'm healing pretty well. Helped Dad in the garage." He pulled up his jogging pants leg and showed her the scar from where the doctor's instrument entered the side of his knee.

She squinted at the tiny red line. "That's it?"

"Yup!" Nick confirmed and rolled down his pant leg.

"I wish your mother would hurry. I'm starving."

Nick patted his belly. "Me too. We found a picture of you and Grandpa." He showed her the photo, and Grandma's eyes got misty and seemed to peer into the distance.

"My lands! That was right before we got married."

"You were a hot chick, Grandma!" Nick winked.

"Hardly." She chuckled. "But your grandfather..." She shook her head, her eyes far away and swimming. "Your grandfather was handsome. And such a good kisser!"

"Grandma!" It was hard for Nick to envision his grandparents having long romantic kisses. His parents, too.

"What else did you find?" Grandma asked, putting the picture on the table.

"An old photo of a civil war soldier." Nick's fingers reached into his pocket for the tin type.

Grandma frowned. "Who?"

"It's hard to tell." He showed her the picture with the stoic boy. Yes, he looked like a boy to Nick.

"Must be one of Grandpa's kin."

"Were we for the south or the north?" For some reason, it felt important for him to understand their allegiance.

"His family was from Kentucky. I'm not sure."

"Kentucky was neutral," Nick's father said when a commercial came on. Nick's father was somewhat of a history buff.

"Dinner!" Nick's mom called.

Nick helped his grandmother from the couch and guided her to the kitchen. It felt good to help others instead of being the invalid.

Chapter 36

I marveled at how well my family had fared while I was gone. I had expected far worse—my children begging for food, my wife haggard and worn.

"William's youngest son helped with the fields until he was called to fight," Emeline explained.

"Why he was just a mite of twelve or thirteen," I said, sharpening a knife and wiping it clean with an old rag.

"Fourteen. We lived off vegetables in the garden and the old hens who took roost in the trees when the Rebels came and took our food." Her face hardened at remembering the pilfering.

"Did they take anything else besides the stock?"

Again, she was quiet as if she was thinking about her answer.

"One old sow was hiding under the porch. A cranky old thing, they let her be."

"Were you or the girls bothered by them?"

Again, Emeline was quiet as she worked the words out in her head. "We hid in the cellar the first time they came." She stopped and seemed to be tasting something sour in her mouth.

"What happened when they came again?" I asked, although my stomach felt tied in knots.

She hung her head. "They didn't bother the girls," she finally said.

"But you...?"

I felt my heart grow cold, and I swallowed slowly, wanting to know what she meant, but I didn't. I should have been here to keep her safe.

I rubbed my knee. "I'm sorry I wasn't here to protect you."

"With a perverted heart devises evil, sowing discord..." Emeline said softly.

"Proverbs. Ah! Yes, they will be punished come judgment day."

I wondered if our Union soldiers had had their way with the Southern women. I hoped we would have acted with more civility.

I wanted to hold her, to love her, but the thought of a Rebel soldier being with her the way a husband and wife should be repulsed me. I felt sick for me, for her, and our family.

Nick awoke shaking. He tried to quell the churning in his stomach and the fever burning his forehead—not an infection. No, this burning was something that came from deep within him. He tried to sleep, but unsettling dreams kept him awake long into the night—visions of a woman fighting off an evil-looking Rebel soldier.

Chapter 37

Nick returned to school, where he and Emily settled into a routine again.

The cafeteria did a robust business after school for anyone needing a snack before sports, music, or school leadership activities. Nick hesitated in the doorway, searching for Emily. Usually, they met on the football bleachers, but with football over and snow on the ground, they had been meeting there since his return to school full-time.

"Hey, a few people are going bowling Saturday night," Emily said after putting a straw in her juice.

"You know my leg hurts," he said and paused. Why had he said that? His words came out before he could think about what he was saying.

He had been able to help Dad in the garage. Why did it start to throb again? He rubbed his knee.

"When did your leg start to hurt again?" she asked. "I thought you were feeling better?"

"I don't know." *The wood rubbed on his stump.*

"I'll put more tar on it and be good to go."

"Tar? A new medicine?" Emily asked, squinting her eyes to study him.

Again, he spoke before thinking about what he said or who said it. He had to think fast. "It looks like tar."

"Oh," she said, gathering up her things.

"Bowling sounds like fun," he said with false

enthusiasm as he reached down again and massaged his thigh. His leg was intact. *Go away, Jonathan*, he warned. *I'm tired of you.*

"I've got to go," she said. "Talk to you later."

****

On Saturday, Nick picked Emily up for bowling, his first time driving a car since his two surgeries. Progress!

They drove to Laketon Lanes, where they met Tiff and Gary. The popular meeting place with a small bowling alley, pizzeria, movie theater, and kiddie arcade was packed. As they entered the front door, a crowd of elementary students ran past, and one plowed into Nick.

"Hey!" he said.

"Sorry!"

Nick rubbed his leg. "At least they didn't hit my bad leg." The scar was minute, but still, it hurt.

Emily and Gary shared a concerned look while Tiffany wandered over to the front desk for shoes.

He rubbed his thigh. "No harm, no foul."

"Come on." Emily dragged him, and Gary followed.

Nick took a size ten and studied the bowling balls. Emily had picked a sparkly green one, and Tiffany was already entering their names on the screen.

Nick hefted up one ball after another, trying to decide the best one to use. Did his incision feel tight?

"You ready?" Emily held her ball to her chest.

"Just about."

She frowned. "What's taking so long?"

"Not sure which one to use. Dr. Garson said I'm not to lift more than ten pounds."

"Oh." Her face crumbled a bit, and she chewed her lip. "Maybe bowling wasn't a good idea."

He didn't want to be that kind of boyfriend who couldn't do anything. "I'll be fine." He gave his chest a rub and felt along the breastbone.

Nick rolled the ball without his usual force. It wobbled in the alley, stayed in the lane, and knocked down three pins.

Next roll, he'd throw a little harder.

"You okay?" Emily asked as she watched his anemic ball-throwing skills.

"Just testing the water."

Nick had the most abysmal scores when they finished three games. Bad scores and all, it felt good to be back with his friends and not at home with his parents. Gary suggested they go into the pizzeria for a snack.

"You call this a snack?" Tiff asked as Gary dug into an extra-large pizza with everything except anchovies. The pizza took up the majority of the table.

"Yup, gotta keep up my strength," Gary said, flexing a bicep at her. Nick nodded in agreement.

Emily rolled her eyes at them, and Nick laughed. It was good to have the easy-going Emily back. He wouldn't make the mistake again of wanting Cat's sexually charged advances over Emily's enduring, sweet love.

Chapter 38

—*I can't wait to see you.*— It was that 541 number again.

He knew it was Cat. Why was she taunting him like a cornered mouse? And why had she sent the "help me" text earlier? Was her nickname taking over her actions? A game of cat and mouse?

"Nick, can you stay after class for a moment?" Coach asked when the bell signaled the end of instruction, and students filed out and down the hall to their lockers or following classes.

Nick hadn't talked one-on-one with the coach since his brief home visit.

"Sure."

"We're starting to plan and get in shape for next year."

"Next year?" Nick asked. He still needed to finish his Christmas shopping for this year!

"Well, yes, next school year."

Nick still didn't get what Coach was trying to say. His blank stare must have tipped Coach off, and he replied, "Football." The coach even raised his brows for emphasis.

"I haven't gotten the okay from my cardiologist to play." The cardiologist sounded so authoritative and unquestionable. "Or for my ACL surgery."

"Of course, you must check with your doctors."

Coach clapped him on the back. "We need you next year, Nick."

The words weighed on him. He didn't like letting anyone down and instead gave Coach a small smile. He wasn't sure he wanted to play football. His heart problem was a good excuse not to play.

He moved to the door. "Gotta go."

"Sure. Sure." The coach waved.

He didn't know how the change had come over him so suddenly. He was a star football player, and in a short time, he wasn't. He could play if he wanted but couldn't muster enough enthusiasm for a weight room workout.

"Nick?" Emily's voice and use of "Nick" confused him and stopped him in his tracks. He should be used to being called "Nick" by now. His breath caught in his throat for one long second, and his mind went blank.

"Nick?" Emily asked again. "What are you doing?"

He glanced around him. He was standing outside Coach's door in the middle of the hall, a stationary object, so other students veered around him.

"Err, nothing." He wiped at his cheeks.

"You have a strange look on your face."

"Thinking." He tapped his forehead.

Bryan plowed into him, knocking him temporarily off balance. "Sorry."

Nick stepped to the side, in no mood to engage Bryan.

"Football," Nick grumbled. "Coach wants me to start working out."

"Can you do that?" Emily asked, touching his arm as they talked.

Probably physically. But mentally… "I dunno."

She frowned. "You love football, don't you?"

He remained quiet and pressed his lips together, contemplating what to say.

"I used to. Everything changed."

Emily's face first registered surprise and then settled into a concentrated stare. "I understand."

But did he?

Chapter 39

While they had gotten a good start on garage cleaning, there was more. Nick peered into the dim interior. It hardly looked like they had accomplished much, except maybe the top of the workbench was cleared. There were still boxes stacked in each corner, lawn furniture cushions, and a crooked Christmas tree they hadn't used in years. Cobwebs decorated the tree—a better Halloween decoration than a Christmas tree. Nick grimaced at the amount of cleaning still needed to finish the job and couldn't use his knee surgery to get out of work.

Nick's father pulled on his work gloves. "Brr, why didn't we finish cleaning the garage in the summer? It's freezing."

"Mom wants it clean before Christmas," Nick said, half listening to his father while turning Coach's voice over and examining his feelings over their "talk after class."

"Are we entertaining guests in the garage?" his father asked, using his best "stand up" comedy voice.

"No," Nick said with a laugh. "You know how she is." He rolled his eyes.

"Do I ever! Get it done, or we'll never hear the end of it!"

Nick glanced around. Was this the best time to talk to his dad about not playing football? He hated to spoil the moment, so he remained quiet. Maybe he could tell Dr. Garson his chest felt tight at his next appointment. Perhaps the doc would say football was out. Yes, an ally would be the best.

Now, he surveyed what they had completed. He had cleaned the workbench and the shelf the last time. His eyes rested on the old nightstand crammed full of stuff.

"Want me to start on this?" He pointed to the small stand. One of the drawers was packed, and he couldn't open the drawer without tugging and pulling.

"Sure, if you can open the drawer," his father said.

For a small piece of furniture, there was a lot of stuff crammed in there. Nick kept pulling papers, books, a musty green bag of some kind, pictures, and a mouse-eaten glove missing all the fingers except the thumb.

"Anything interesting?" his father called.

"Whose nightstand was this?"

"Your grandparents', I think." The light wood didn't match anything in their house.

Nick picked up the green bag. "What's this?"

His father came over, wiping his brow on his sleeve, and frowned at the tag on the handle. "I think this was Grandpa's duffle bag from the war."

It smelled of dirt, dust, and age—a hard thing to describe. And to emphasize his feelings, Nick sneezed. His father turned the bag inside out, and a piece of paper fluttered to the floor.

Nick picked up the scrap. "Hey!" He lifted the paper and read. "Looks like an address." Elm. Paducah.

He handed the smudged and dirty paper to his father. "I don't think we know anyone in Paducah."

The word labored over his tongue—a mouthful, to be sure.

"Where is Paducah?"

"Ohio?" His father guessed. Nick wasn't sure he knew either.

The state name was smudged and unrecognizable.

"Maybe someone Grandpa knew in the war?"

"Could be. We might never know."

"Do you think Grandma would?" Nick asked.

"Possibly."

"I'll ask next time she's over."

Nick put the paper back in the knapsack and began sorting through the old newspaper clippings, a package of gum chewed on by mice, and greeting cards, tossing most in the trash. The cobweb ladened Christmas tree was dismantled and dumped into the garbage. Nick wiped his hands on the back of his jeans, happy to stop working. There was room for one car in the two-stall garage now.

Chapter 40

Nick had progressed from weekly sessions with Dr. Patar to every other week. Soon, once a month would certainly suffice. He was scheduled to see her today after school, but before he left for the day, Coach caught him in the hallway.

"Some of the guys are lifting weights after school tonight. You free?"

"No, sorry, I have a doctor's appointment." Nick kept his eyes down and studied the scuffs on the floor. He liked Mr. Sullivan as a teacher and as a football coach. He was letting him down, but it couldn't be helped. Nick couldn't get excited about football like he once had.

"Have you asked about resuming strength training?"

Nick looked up briefly. "No, I will when I see Dr. Garson again."

"Okay, see you tomorrow." Coach gave him a brief upturning of his lips before patting Nick's shoulder and giving him a look Nick couldn't discern before heading toward the weight rooms.

Emily clasped him around the waist and smiled up at him. "What's going on?"

"Coach wants me to start working out for football next year."

Emily frowned. "Are you supposed to do that?"

Exactly. Emily understood, but why didn't anyone else?

Nick kissed Emily goodbye with a promise of a call before leaving to see the psychologist.

"Hi, Nick, come in." Dr. Patar peered critically at him. "Any changes?"

Why was she looking at him oddly? Did he have something on him? He wiped at his face.

"I didn't mean to suggest anything was wrong," she explained when he voiced his concern. "You look happier than I recall when we first started seeing each other."

"Things are going pretty well." He made a slicing motion with his hand to indicate all was calm.

"Pretty good. Define that for me?"

"I'm doing well in school, back with my girlfriend." He made fluttering motions with his fingers about his relationship with Em. "Helping my parents at home."

She inclined her head. "Good to hear. What about the other personalities we talked about previously?"

"Jean Claude has disappeared." He snapped his fingers. "Gone." Jean Claude had left Nick's life in shambles and then died.

"And why do you think he left?"

"I don't think there was anything else to discover. I didn't leave Chaton to die, as Cat said. Jean Claude died trying to save her. Nothing else to know."

She flipped through her notes. "What about Jonathan?"

"He hasn't left." Nick made a face.

"So one personality stayed, whereas the other left?"

"Yeah." He didn't know which personality was worse, Jean Claude or Jonathan. Both were different and the same.

"Tell me what you know about Jonathan thus far," she asked.

Nick studied the ceiling as he pushed his thoughts in order. "He was a soldier." He tapped a finger on the chair. "He's married with two little girls and lives on a farm. He has one leg. He lost it in the war." Both men were reluctant to fight. Jean Claude was a student, and Jonathan wanted to care for his crops and animals.

"When does Jonathan come to visit you?"

Nick studied the ceiling again as if it held the answers instead of a fluorescent light that cast yellow shadows over everything. He remembered the times Jonathan intruded on his life when they went to the dance, bowling, and after. "All different times," Nick said. Jonathan mainly appeared in his dreams at night. "When I've been active."

"Interesting. Why do you think that?"

He didn't know the answer, but "he couldn't do those things with one leg" popped out of his mouth.

"Have you been able to push him aside when he intrudes in your life?"

"Sometimes, but usually after I've said something that sounds all wrong. My parents are sympathetic, but I haven't shared anything with my girlfriend or best friend."

"I see."

"He has many problems but seems like a nice guy."

"So there's no predictable pattern to this alter?"

"Nope."

"Hmmm." She drummed her fingers on her desk.

"Usually, they appear when there has been some trauma or stress, but you say this isn't the case?"

"Yup."

"Just out of the blue?" She paused. "Can you give me an example?"

He guessed it wasn't quite that simple. He seemed to dream of Jonathan more often since Cat began texting about returning to Laketon.

Dr. Patar waited and inclined her head.

Nick cleared his throat and continued, "I went bowling and kept thinking—I only had one leg. It's hard to bowl that way. My friends have been great, but they sometimes look at me strangely."

"I can imagine."

Nick clenched his fingers on the armrest. Maybe he wasn't a simple case of DID. Could it be he was reincarnated, and the Bible was wrong? Neither DID nor reincarnation was ideal. He blew out his breath and wished the dreams would go away and he could go on with his life.

Chapter 41

"Guess who I ran into at the grocery store," his father said when Nick returned from seeing Dr. Patar.

It could be any number of people, including his third-grade teacher.

"Coach Sullivan! He's excited about next year's season and all the seniors returning."

Nick remained quiet and chewed absently on his lower lip.

His father continued, not noticing Nick's silence or how he shifted his feet. "He was wondering when you could start to work out and put on some of the muscle you lost during your hospital stays."

"I haven't talked to Dr. Garson about working out again."

"I bet he'll say it's fine! He seemed to think it wouldn't be a problem last time we talked." His father clasped Nick's shoulder.

It hurt being tackled and slammed to the ground with a pile of guys on top—sometimes, it was even hard to breathe.

"I don't want to hurt myself or undo the patch on my heart when someone tackles me."

"Understandable," his father said, finally looking directly at him.

"I'm worried about playing football again," Nick admitted. "I already told Coach I might not be playing."

"You know, if you don't play your senior year, you won't get into college."

"I know. I considered that." Nick grabbed a fistful of hair. "I also have to take care of myself," he pointed out.

"I'll be disappointed," his father said, his concerned look replaced with sadness. "But I understand."

"I'll talk to Dr. Garson. I'm not doing anything until I have his A-okay."

His father squeezed his shoulder again. "We'll be proud of you whether you play football or not."

Nick winced internally at the squeeze. He was really out of shape if that hurt. "Thanks." It did feel good to have some of the weight lifted.

****

The next day during World History, as Nick was making his way down the aisle to his seat, suddenly his leg gave out under him, and he went sprawling over the desk, feeling a hot pulsing pain in his leg, enough to bring tears to his eyes.

Nick touched his leg gingerly. The place next to his knee where he had the ACL surgery felt hot, with a knot growing under the skin. He froze, his body rigid and his face grimaced with pain.

Coach rushed toward him. "What's wrong?"

"I don't know," he moaned. Nick felt sweat pour down his face, and he managed to move his chin up and down, his teeth and lips clamped together in agony.

"Someone go to the office and call for an ambulance," Coach said. One of the girls by the door ran out.

"Steady." Coach reached his hand out. "What

happened?"

"I don't…know." Nick pushed off the desk, and when he did, he was out of breath and panting. The pain in his leg didn't feel the same as the ligament tear. This pain was hot and pulsing, whereas the incision stung, and he couldn't put any pressure on his leg.

Soon Nick heard a commotion in the hall as the paramedics arrived and transported him to the waiting ambulance.

Emily rushed to his side. "Oh, my gosh! I just heard!"

He flinched at the pain as part of his jeans was cut away. "My leg is on fire! Call my…" Nick gritted his teeth at the pain, tried to concentrate on the flashing lights then felt the blood pressure cuff tighten on his arm. "Parents, would you?"

"I will!" Emily rushed to the office, probably to use their phone.

He was loaded into the waiting ambulance and given oxygen.

"Relax, we'll be there soon."

Nick tried to relax, but his mind refused to settle, shuffling through all the possible scenarios.

At the hospital, his harried and worried-looking parents met him in the emergency room. His scan revealed a clot, so he was hooked up to intravenous medicine to break down the block, which could require surgery.

He overheard one of the nurses talking. A clot could break loose at any time and go to his heart or brain, so he'd be monitored closely. Nick knew that meant he'd get little rest.

There would be no talk about playing football or getting in shape until the clot was gone.

Chapter 42

After a breakfast of cinnamon sugar toast and porridge, we filed out to plant the corn fields.

I wobbled behind my tiny daughters. Emeline led the way with her pregnant belly. She dug the holes, the girls dropped in the seeds, and I limped behind, covering each hole with a swipe of my crutch. Usually, I'd lead the planting party, but now Emeline did the honors.

As we worked, I flashed back to another cornfield—this one someplace in Tennessee. The field was ready for harvesting, but the farm appeared deserted. I picked some corn before the wagons, horses, and cannons trampled the rest. I wasn't sure where I was. The days and nights blurred into one. War did that to a man, reducing him to a killing machine, his insides gone and replaced by ice water and a chilled heart.

"Daddy?"

I was jerked back from that other cornfield to this one, my own.

"You missed some."

"That I did." I smiled at my daughter and patted her bonneted head.

We planted the rows with three giant steps between each seed. The plants needed space to grow.

I stopped and wiped my sweaty brow. Even in early spring, the temperatures fluctuated between 60 and 70 degrees. The mild weather was a welcome respite after the freezing temperatures of winter.

Emeline, with her hair tucked under a bonnet, wore an apron to hold the seeds. The girls resembled miniatures of their mama with their aprons and bonnets. All three worked to plant the seeds at least an inch deep. I followed their bobbing bonnets, wishing the girls could go to school.

Stormy scampered after the girls—her coat was glossy from feasting on the barn mice. They bent to pet the cat, who intertwined herself around their legs.

Emeline stopped and rubbed the small of her back. "Girls! Leave the cat alone."

"She's so pretty and soft," Sophia said. "Why can't we pet her?"

"Cats have lice," Emeline snapped.

"Yes, Mama."

Stormy stopped and raised her tail, the hair bristled out. I scanned the fields and spotted something—a man crouched down. From the looks of him, he appeared to be a Rebel with a tattered gray coat. The man stood unsteadily and came toward us— his eyes black pupils of pain and anger. I pushed the girls behind me.

"Go! You're not wanted here!" I said in my most commanding voice, but the man lurched forward.

He had a holstered pistol, but that was his only weaponry I could tell. With some difficulty he pulled out the weapon.

I had no weapons, only my crutch, but I needed it to stay upright.

"What do you want?" I asked.

"Food!"

I studied on the man. Did he mean to harm us? He looked malnourished and injured. Would he only want a meal and to be on his way? As he got closer, I saw the leer in his eyes when he beheld Sophia. I pushed her behind me when he made to grab her. I leaned against my wooden leg and swung my crutch at him. He looked at me in surprise and kicked at my wooden leg. I landed on the ground, and he stood on unsteady legs and lifted the pistol. Stormy hissed and jumped on his leg, and he let out a yelp before shaking his leg. The distraction allowed me to kick out with my right leg, knocking him off balance, and I swung the crutch like a club and caught him square in the temple. I saw the look of surprise on his face before his eyes rolled back and he slumped to the ground.

"Quick!" I said. "Give me something to tie his hands." With some difficulty I picked up the pistol and put it in my pocket. Emeline had torn off a strip of her apron. "You'll have to tie his hands."

She managed to turn him, but then stopped and looked at me.

"What is it?"

"I think he's dead," she said, feeling the pulse on his neck.

I didn't like her touching him that way.

"Then I guess we bury him," I said. The sights I had seen on the battlefield had hardened my soul.

"Daddy!" Anne tugged on my overalls. "Stormy saved us!"

"That she did. She warned us of danger."

Emeline's face softened.

"Animals are right smart."

Stormy wound her way around our legs before

Sophia petted her and told her, "You're a good kitty, Stormy!"

Emeline frowned at my coveralls. "You're bleeding."

"That I am." The fall must have irritated my stump. My leg burned, but I turned to the task at hand. "We'll need to dig a hole."

We did. Right in the middle of the cornfield lay a dead Confederate soldier fertilizing our crop.

Chapter 43

When the clot dissolved and Nick didn't require surgery, they released him from the hospital. He returned to school two days later. Now he swung up and down the hallways on crutches and was advised to keep his leg elevated. When Nick got to World History, Coach cleared the way for him down the aisle, pushing backpacks and purses out of the way. Nick put his leg up on the seat in front of him.

He leaned back in the chair in class, folded his arms, and listened to Coach talk about the Middle East conflict. When Coach finished, and the class ended, he came over to Nick. "How are you feeling after your hospital stay?" Coach's eyes were narrow with concern.

"Better." Nick thought Coach was leading up to lifting weights and getting in shape, so he said, "I still haven't seen my cardiologist yet. I've got weights at home." A set they had uncovered in the garage covered in cobwebs and dust, looking ancient with rust.

"Okay, remember there's a spot for you on the team next year."

"Thanks!"

He would never play football again. He had just enough strength to plant his fields. He envisioned rows of corn, not an unfamiliar sight in rural Laketon, but the scene in his mind didn't resemble anything around here. He shook himself mentally and peered down at his legs.

He had two working appendages!

Once in the hallway between classes, Nick checked his phone. Another message from that 541 number:

—*We're on our way back to Michigan.*—

—*Who is this?*— Even as he typed those words, he knew who it was—or thought he knew.

—*You don't know? Then you'll be in for a surprise.*—

Shit. Nick rubbed at the tense muscles on the back of his neck and moved his shoulders around.

"What are you doing?" Emily asked when Nick finished texting and went to his locker.

"Getting ready for the next class."

"I saw you texting someone."

"My mom."

No use getting Emily upset about Cat's return. Part of him wanted to see her, but a part, okay, fifty-one percent didn't. His love life was predictable when Cat was gone. Things could get complicated again.

Chapter 44

The corn was almost a foot high and stalks over the dead Confederate soldier's body were robust and healthy. I wondered about his kin folk, if they pondered what had happened to him. The same thing could have happened to me, but I was spared death. We were preparing for the new baby. Hopefully, a little boy to help with the farm tasks.

Emeline was in the kitchen making bread for the morning. The girls were playing with a string of yarn, making Stormy pounce. They giggled at the cat's antics, rolling around and batting the yarn.

All was right, I decided. I whittled as Sophia and Anne sang to the cat:

"Miss Mary Mack Mack Mack
All dressed in black, black, black
With silver buttons, buttons, buttons
All down her back, back, back."

Emeline peeked around the door at the trio by the fire and smiled.

"Come and sit a spell, Mother," I said with love.

She shook her head and gave me a tired smile before returning to her bread-making. We would be glad to have fresh bread in the morning. Stormy, tired of playing with the yarn, scampered after Emeline into the kitchen.

I had never heard that song about Mary Mack

before. My favorite while marching along was:
The Union forever,
Hurrah! boys, hurrah!
Down with the traitors,
Up with the stars;
While we rally round the flag, boys,
Rally once again.
I hummed it under my breath as I continued making the figure of a pig. The girls left, and I was alone. I again lapsed into my memories of marching and the camaraderie with the other soldiers.

Presently I heard a scream, "Help me! Please! Fire!"

I jerked away from my whittling and remembering. With some difficulty, I pushed to standing, took my crutches, and went into the kitchen. I froze momentarily at the sight of Emeline engulfed in flames. My training kicked in, and I knocked her to the floor and commanded, "Roll! Roll!"

She did with some difficulty, her skirts hindering her.

I swung over to the sink, hoisted the bucket of water, and managed to douse the flames. I could tell by the blackened, curling, and bubbling skin that Emeline was severely burned. And the smell of burned flesh assailed me with memories of the war anew.

I bent over the best I could, leaning against the table and using my crutch to steady me to get a closer look.

"What happened?"

She was having trouble speaking—her lips blackened. "The... The... That cat."

I glanced around. Surely she didn't mean Stormy,

who sat calmly watching us, licking her paws without a care in the world.

Kerosene fingers reached out from the overturned lantern. I could see the fire's path, burning the bread dough and then Emeline.

"Can you stand?" I knew I wouldn't be able to lift her myself.

"I...I think...so." With difficulty, she got to her hands and knees and then stood with the help of the table.

It was good the whole house hadn't caught fire.

"Get...the...cat...out!" Emeline managed to say, her words muffled from grotesquely swollen lips.

My daughters stood frozen in the doorway, their eyes fixed on their mama.

I couldn't fathom how the cat figured in the fire. For some particular reason, Emeline didn't like Stormy.

"I've seen paint used on burns," I said mainly to myself. Emeline moaned. "I'll get some from the barn. You get to bed."

She clutched her shifting belly—the baby! Was it coming? There would be no time to summon the midwife.

First things first. To help Emeline.

"Anne, you stay with your mama. Sophia, come with me. You can carry the paint. Hurry! We have to help her!"

Chapter 45

Nick and Emily helped prepare the church for the Christmas Eve service. Nick propped his crutch beside his chair, as he and Emily put little paper wheels around the bottom of each candle so they wouldn't drip wax.

"Thanks for helping me," Nick said. They put the completed candles in boxes for easy distribution on Christmas Eve.

"I like spending time with you," she said, giving him a shy smile.

"Me too."

"Can I be your girl again?" She chewed on her bottom lip.

"You've always been my girl." Nick reached over and squeezed her hand.

"Even when that bitch stole you away from me?"

"She didn't have my heart," he said and patted his chest. Damn, he was poetic this afternoon. It was true. Cat had a part of him. Not his heart but something more sensual. But love? He didn't think so.

"How many of these do we need to make?" Emily asked, eyeing the boxes of candles with paper skirts stacked in a neat pile.

"All of them."

"How many people are coming tonight?"

"We're usually packed." Nick remembered several Christmas Eve services where people were standing at the back. He mentally envisioned about two hundred people packed into the pews.

Anyone and everyone came out on this magical night of the holy birth. Nick loved Christmas Eve. Afterward, they roasted marshmallows at home and made s'mores on the fire in the living room—good memories of Christmas past.

A memory flitted across his brain of a different Christmas. A fireplace, but using a tin pan popping corn over the fire. And when the girls were asleep, putting sweets and mittens in their stockings hung from the mantel. Nick blinked. Jonathan's Christmas.

When Nick and Emily finished putting the candles and holders together, Em said, "I better go home. I have more wrapping to do."

Nick hadn't even thought about wrapping. He had something for Em and his parents in bags in his closet.

"Me too," he said.

"See you later?"

They leaned together for a kiss and just stayed there. It felt good to feel Emily's lips on his. He felt a stirring in his belly, so he pulled away and looked up at the cross that shadowed them. Now was not the time or place for more than just a kiss. Nick needed to get home and change before the service started in a couple of hours.

****

Besides the abundance of candles—the church, decorated with giant wreaths on the windows, had its altar draped in a white and gold cloth. Poinsettias lined the partition in front of the choir, and they sang "Oh Come All Ye Faithful" as the worshipers filed in, stamping the snow from their boots, stowing their coats,

172

and greeting friends and neighbors.

Emily supported his grandmother up the steps and helped her with her coat.

Grandma eyed Nick. "You sure are accident-prone. Always have been. Falling from trees, stitches, surgery, and now this." She waved toward his leg as he leaned on a single crutch.

True. But he responded with, "Merry Christmas, Grandma" instead.

He guided Grandma toward the front of the church to sit by his mother. Nick and Em would sit near the back and hand out programs as people came in for the service.

When the service was underway, members came to the front of the church to read parts of the Christmas story. The old familiar carols were sung and enjoyed. And Emily was by his side. He glanced over at her and smiled, and she back at him. "I'm glad you're here," he whispered, cupping her hand in his.

As the service drew to a close, his mother and Emily helped pass out the candles for "Silent Night." When everyone had a lit candle, they began singing. Nick held his candle to Emily's for a spark.

Then over the organ music, Nick felt cold air flood the church when the large double doors opened with a swish, knocking him into Emily.

He heard Emily gasp as a shadowy figure strode up the aisle. Nick couldn't tell if they were male or female because of the full-length black coat with a hood. A shadowy demonic apparition continued toward Reverend Dupont. Nick's father stood frozen behind the pulpit. All talking and music stopped. The ghost of Christmas past came to haunt him. A whisper began at the back of the church. "Cat. That's the girl. The one who…"

Nick heard a strangled gasp from Emily, turned toward her, and saw her sleeve on fire. Nick gaped at the flames taking hold of her sleeve and used his hand to stop them, scorching his palm, but they had a mind of their own and continued eating greedily at the material of her dress.

Emily's eyes were wild with pain and confusion, as she gasped, "Fire!"

"Drop and roll!" He shoved her to the floor.

Several people handed Nick bottles of water, and he was able to douse the flames from turning Em into a living candle.

People crowded around, and Emily sat up, cradling her arm. Nick held out his hand for her and saw her sleeve had a brown stain, and she smelled of burnt fabric.

The shadowy figure stopped by them. "Surprise!" Cat exclaimed, pushing back her hood and revealing her face.

Nick stared at her dully. What was she doing here?

"Are you okay?" Cat leaned over. "I hope he hasn't hurt you!"

"No!" Emily cringed, tears in her eyes. "He would never hurt me."

Nick looked from Cat to Emily, watching the exchange with growing dread—not for the here and now. A feeling deep inside him knew this had something to do with Jonathan.

Nick watched Cat make her way toward his father.

"I'm sorry I disrupted the service," Cat said.

Nick couldn't hear his father's response because of

the whispers of the rest of the church. Besides he needed to give his full attention to Emily.

She whispered and gave a forced smile. "I don't think I'm burned too bad." She inspected her arm, turning it back and forth.

"Does it hurt?" Nick asked.

"A little. Sort of stings," she said.

A picture of a woman, half charred beyond recognition, raced across Nick's mind, and as much as he pushed at it, it didn't retreat.

"I'm sorry she's back," Nick whispered.

"Why can't she leave you alone?" Emily whispered back.

The million-dollar question.

"Everyone all right?" Reverend Dupont asked, coming toward them with Cat and Grandma trailing behind.

"A little mishap," Grandma said. "It's out now." But Grandma's eyes sparkled like the commotion was the most exciting event ever. She'd have something to retell to her Bunco group back at the Manor.

The church was in disarray—everyone pushing to see Emily's arm. This service was officially over for this Christmas Eve.

Bryan muscled his way toward them and smiled at Emily. "I hope you'll be okay?"

She nodded but didn't look at him. "Merry Christmas." Bryan squeezed Emily's hand and turned to Nick. "You too."

A lackluster holiday greeting, but Bryan was trying to be friendly, Nick reasoned.

Nick's mouth seemed to hang from his jaw, and he didn't say anything until Emily elbowed him. "Uh, yeah, nice to see you," he mumbled unenthusiastically. "Merry Christmas."

The first aid kit was located, and Emily's wrist was treated and bandaged. Cat's return wasn't a good omen, and Nick felt his stomach fill with dread.

Chapter 46

The evening would have been perfect except for the burned sleeve incident. Nick's palm tingled, and tiny blisters dotted the skin. His mother had given him some cream, but still, it stung, an irritating reminder of Cat's presence in the church.

He shook away his dark thoughts and concentrated on their tradition of roasting marshmallows and making s'mores on Christmas Eve. He relished the ritual as his father tended the flickering flames, and they pulled their chairs closer.

"What are you thankful for this year, Nick?" his mother asked.

"Lots of things. My health—" He looked at his mom, then his dad. "—and family."

"That's what I'm thankful for, too," his mother added. "And to have Grandma still with us."

"Mmm hmm," Nick agreed. "Dad?"

"I'm thankful the Lions aren't in last place!"

Nick and his mother laughed at his humor attempt after the somber church service.

"I'm glad we can celebrate together as a family and Jesus's birth," his father said, his tone turned serious.

Nick put two marshmallows on the metal skewer and turned it slowly, browning it on all sides. He watched the flames jump and surge, sparking like fireflies in the darkness. His mind went to the cold and hungry soldiers sitting by the fire, warming their hands, bellies empty. He could imagine what *those starving boys would have given for chocolate, marshmallow, and graham cracker treats.*

"Happy for the warm fire and grub," Nick said.

His mother laughed. "Grub? S'mores are now called grub?"

Jonathan's thoughts had tangled up with his again.

"I agree, good grub." His father nodded.

"Not always," Nick said, poking at the fire with his skewer.

"I see," she said.

His father stood, patted Nick's shoulder, went into the kitchen, and returned with two glasses of wine. His parents sat sipping their drinks while Nick continued to prod the fire, his mind going in a million different directions—the burnt sleeve, the memories of the battlefield Christmas, and mostly, Cat's untimely return.

It was almost eleven p.m., and Nick yawned. He wanted to put out his presents for his parents and Emily before he turned in. He had bought Emily a necklace with two hearts intertwined, meaning friends or commitment? He wasn't sure what it meant.

Minnie curled around his legs before settling by the fire. Her coat shimmered in the light.

Chapter 47

Christmas morning was always fun, Nick thought as he crept down the stairs, using the handrail for support. His mother and father had been busy. His parents must have stayed up late, filling the area around the tree with presents. His mother was wearing a Christmas sweatshirt that lit up with twinkling lights. Nick gave his mother a grimace when she pointed to her shirt.

"You don't like my shirt?"

He yawned. "It's too early." But he paused and lifted his nose to smell cinnamon rolls baking in the oven. His father was gone, but he was probably picking up Grandma to spend the day with them.

His mother was sipping coffee while Minnie purred contentedly at her side. "Merry Christmas."

He leaned over and hugged her.

"Looks like elves visited us," Nick said, calculating what could be in the different-sized boxes and bags. The only thing he had asked for was new speakers.

"Appears so," his mother said, a sly half-smile on her lips.

Nick left the tree and helped himself to coffee.

His father returned with Grandma. "Merry Christmas!"

"Can I get you some coffee?" Nick offered.

"Sure!" Grandma said. "Lots of cream." His father

took her coat, and she sat by the fire, warming her hands.

Nick poured her a cup and added a large dollop of cream before joining them by the tree. Nick lifted his nose and sniffed the air—cinnamon, pine, and coffee. His mother was baking sweet rolls, and his stomach did a little happy dance.

Later, after the gifts were opened and the mess cleaned up from the paper and wrappings, Emily arrived bearing her gifts. The sleeve of her sweater covered her burned arm.

"Hi!"

Emily was a favorite with Nick's parents and grandmother. Heck, she was liked by almost everyone. Nick was lucky she was by his side still. He didn't want to screw it up again.

Nick's grandmother eagerly unwrapped Emily's box. Inside were fudge, cookies, and bread.

"My mom, sisters, and I have been baking a storm," Emily explained.

Grandma popped a piece of fudge in her mouth. "Just the way I like it! Sweet and melts in your mouth." She grinned, revealing chocolate-covered teeth. "Thank you!"

Emily gave the same gift to his parents.

And as if reading Nick's mind, his mother said, "Will you help me in the kitchen?" She nodded at his father and grandmother.

"I don't…" his grandmother started to say, until Nick's mother tugged on her sleeve and raised her brows toward Nick and Emily.

They left them alone. Nick leaned in and kissed Em before handing her the box with the necklace.

When she opened it, her face registered surprise and happiness. "I love it, Nick! It's beautiful!" she gushed. "I want to wear it. I don't ever want to take it off!" She quickly swept her hair up and let Nick fasten the clasp. "How does it look?"

He leaned over and kissed her. "Very nice." He cocked his head at her, studying her eyes and seeing caring reflected, and kissed her again. For this kiss, he took his time.

His phone vibrated in his pocket. When he finished kissing Emily, he glanced at the caller. Cat.

"Is that from her?" Emily asked, frowning at the unknown area code.

"Spam," he said.

He'd call Cat back later or, maybe, never. Nick knew he had to talk to her, though. They were tied together because of events many years ago. Although the Jean Claude and Chaton saga was over, there was Jonathan to contend with. How did Cat fit in there?

Chapter 48

"Mommy!" Anne threw herself on the bed, jiggling Emeline and making her shriek.

"Anne, stop with that!" I admonished. "Your ma's real bad off."

Emeline watched through pain-filled eyes. "I swear the cat knocked over the lantern." She moaned.

"Stormy didn't mean it!" Anne whined.

I patted her head. "She knows that." I touched Emeline's shoulder and picked up the paint and a rag. "Let's get you feeling better."

We used paint to cool the wounds in the army. For bad burns, it kept body fluids in. I hoped it would work this time. Just then, Sophia walked in with tears in her eyes and asked, "Will you take Stormy away?"

"No, she can stay in the barn where she belongs."

Anne sniffed. "She didn't mean it."

"I know she didn't. Why don't you take Stormy to the barn and make her a bed of straw to sleep in?"

They nodded and left me to tend to Emeline.

"This might hurt," I said to Emeline when the girls left. "But I've got to clean the wound."

She nodded.

I handed her the end of the quilt. "Here. Bite on this."

I pulled away the clothing stuck to her skin. She shrieked, and Anne ran back in.

"Daddy? What's wrong!"

"Stay out there with your sister while I get your mother fixed up. Can you bring me the emergency whiskey?"

Anne brought the whiskey. I opened my wife's lips and poured some into her mouth. "Swallow," I commanded. I nudged her lips apart again. "Take another." I looked at her eyes to judge if the drink had taken effect, and when her lids looked heavy, I began to paint the burned areas.

Chapter 49

Nick realized he had been holding his breath figuratively during the holidays, waiting. Waiting for Cat to turn up unexpectedly—like at church—and wreak havoc on his relationship with Emily. He needed to talk with Cat, but he dreaded it.

So he texted her.

—Why did you send me the help message?—

—I needed help.—

—Why?—

—I was kidnapped.—

—What!!!!!!—

—Can you come over?—

—No, Emily might see my car.—

—Her again?—

—How about at Del's Diner?—

"I'm going out for a bit," Nick told his mother as he put on his jacket and gloves to scrape off the snow from his car. He had progressed from crutches to a cane, and now, he was walking on his own. Sometimes he limped for no reason, and when he noticed what he was doing, he stopped.

Getting rid of the snow was more manageable with his increased mobility.

His mother frowned, her hands busy mixing and rolling out meatballs for the New Year's Day open house they had had for as long as Nick could remember.

"I was hoping you could take some of this food to the church?" The kitchen smelled of meatballs—onion, garlic, and meat.

Nick's stomach grumbled. Maybe he'd have a burger at Del's. "I won't be long."

She turned back to the meatballs she was browning on the stove. Nick wasn't sure where his father was, but as Nick was cleaning the snow from his car, he came around the corner carrying a snow shovel.

"You going someplace?"

"To talk to Cat." Honesty was the best policy.

"Aah," his father said as he began knocking icicles off the roof with the shovel.

Nick finished warming up and cleaning off his car and went to meet Cat. While he drove, he had one eye out for Emily's car, but thankfully, she wasn't out on this snowy day.

Del's Diner was from the 1950s and had been a favorite place for students to eat after a date. It had been around since Nick's parents were teens. The servers wore skirts with poodles on them and two-tone shoes.

Nick parked next to Cat's green Jag and went into the diner. The bell chimed, and as unobtrusively as he could, he looked into the booths to see if he knew anyone. *Whew*! No one from school. Cat was sitting at the last table, and Nick slid in on the other side.

She looked the same. Had it been almost three months since she left? It seemed like years with his heart defect, ACL surgery, and learning about Jonathan.

"Why are you limping?" she asked—same old Cat.

Her comment caused him to pause. Yes, why was he limping? Habit? Soreness?

"Tore my ACL and had it fixed," Nick said, running his hand along his leg before looking at the menu. He felt her eyes on him and set the menu aside. Del's had a limited selection which he knew by heart.

They continued to watch each other when a waitress came over. "What can I get you?"

Nick ordered a burger and cola, and Cat ordered a salad.

When the waitress left, Nick whispered, "Kidnapped?" His brows rose, waiting for her response.

She nodded and toyed with the silverware. "A gang was kidnapping girls in Roseview."

"How did you get away?" Nick asked.

"I had to fight my way out of the trunk. My brother and his friend came for me."

Wait! Cat had never mentioned a brother before. "You never told me you had a brother."

She shrugged. "I'm not sure exactly, but we look a lot alike, so people in school assumed we were related."

"So you don't know for sure?" He frowned as the waitress set down his cola and water for Cat.

"As I said, I'm not exactly positive, but there's a large Roma population in Oregon, and I was adopted. It's possible." She moved one shoulder as if she didn't care.

He unwrapped his straw. "Why were they kidnapping girls?"

"There's a large cartel of Romas in Europe who pay good money for Roma women."

Nick stopped, his hand hovering near his drink.

"Were you tied up?"

She sighed. "No, but I used my dance training to kick them."

Nick whistled. "Sounds like a spy movie or something."

"It was something all right." Cat's eyes looked away from him. "My parents and friends and the police were looking for me." She took a sip of water. "I couldn't wait to get back here—" She cleared her throat. "—to see you."

"Emily and I are back together." Nick jutted his chin out. The words seemed like a heavy stone tossed in the water, sinking fast.

"You couldn't wait for me?"

"Cat…"

She leaned forward but sat back as the waitress arrived with his burger and her salad.

Nick stared dully at his food, suddenly not as hungry as he had been.

"There was never any 'us,' " he said.

"There was! It was just starting."

Nick shook his head as he answered. "Jean Claude has gone away. The psychologist I'm seeing says I have Dissociative Identity Disorder, not reincarnation."

Cat made a face. "Of course, that's what they would say! It's an easy diagnosis, and one people understand. Most people are uncomfortable with the idea of reincarnation."

The bell on the door chimed, and several people came in. Nick ducked down when a freshman girl and an older woman sat near them.

No more talk about reincarnation. The last thing Nick needed was that rumor going around the school. He already felt like a somewhat outcast with his surgeries and strange utterances.

Chapter 50

Nick drove home, his mind reeling from his conversation with Cat. Nothing had been decided, and he hadn't been forceful with her to forget about them so he could be with Emily. He worried about what was said and also what wasn't said.

He had little time to worry because his parents always had a New Year's Day open house for friends, parishioners, and neighbors. Tomorrow was New Year's Day, and everyone was in high gear. They didn't hold the festivities at the church but in the old farmhouse, so neighbors who didn't attend their church could come.

Every year, Nick was expected to help—his job was to move mountains of food. The food was stored in the church's industrial-sized refrigerator. Tables and chairs from the church were brought over, cleaned, and set up.

New Year's Day was still and cold. The roads were mainly clear, with small patches of snow and no major storms to hinder the guests. The parish house, located on the outskirts of Laketon, had been a former farm. Their house was a giant rambling white clapboard with a wide front porch and shutters—a typical midwestern, out-in-the-country home.

Nick and Emily spent all morning transporting crockpots full of meatballs and bowls of potato salad back from the church's refrigerators.

"Your mother has enough food for an army," Emily said, standing and arching her back.

"She's been cooking up a storm. Driving me crazy. I've snuck a few meatballs when she wasn't looking."

Emily poked him. "You're bad!" She laughed.

"Food drives me crazy!" He grabbed her, twirled her around, and limped back to the counter, panting.

Nick's mother served the same things each year: meatballs, potato salad, coleslaw, and beans, and had ordered an enormous sheet cake welcoming in the new year.

When they deposited the last round of food in the kitchen, Nick jumped in the shower, then changed into a nice sweater and slacks.

Their living room and kitchen were packed when the party got into motion. Grandma held the place of honor in the oversized recliner Nick's dad watched football from. Nick checked to see if she needed anything before squeezing around Bryan, who was blocking the table holding the water, coffee, and sodas.

"Excuse me, Bryan."

"Sorry," Bryan said. He was on his best behavior with his parents by his side. And Nick's grandma was seated nearby.

"You're Bryan?" Grandma asked.

"Yup."

"A friend of Nick's?"

Nick remained in earshot. How would Bryan respond?

"Sort of."

"Ha!" She laughed.

Nick grinned inwardly. Grandma was a shrewd

judge of people.

Bryan's face colored. "We've had our differences."

Bryan's mother elbowed Bryan. "You used to be friends when you were younger."

"That was a long time ago, Mother," Bryan grumbled.

Nick found Gary and Tiffany squeezed in a corner, balancing their plates of food on their laps.

"Your mom sure knows how to cook!" Gary said, then added his signature low whistle. "Good grub."

Nick would have to agree with Gary, but so far, he hadn't been able to sit down and enjoy the food beyond what he had sampled here and there.

Emily had been helping him refill food bowls and making sure people had drinks. Nick noticed Bryan had tried to talk to her, but she brushed by him.

He was about to take his first bite when the doorbell rang. Nick put his plate down and watched as Cat stood in the doorway, dressed in all black. All talking seemed to have stopped when Cat, wearing over-the-knee four-inch heeled boots, stepped through the door.

"Well, well," Gary whispered. "Look what the cat dragged in!"

Tiffany elbowed him. What was Cat doing here? Nick stood speechless by Emily's side. His hand grew clammy in hers.

Emily whispered loud enough for Nick to hear, "I guess my New Year's Resolution won't come true."

"Cat!" Nick's father said. "What a surprise!"

Cat accepted a hug from Nick's parents.

Nick, remembering his manners, finally uprooted his granite-like feet and plodded to where Cat was standing. Emily trailed behind him. "Hi. Happy New Year." His greeting was anything but happy.

"I need to talk to you. Alone," Cat whispered.

Nick heard Emily's noisy intake of breath.

He mumbled something noncommittal. "More?" *They had just met at the restaurant yesterday. What was so important now? Was Cat needling Emily again?*

"Help yourself to food," Nick's mother said.

"Thank you. I remember your delicious cooking, Mrs. Dupont."

"Please, call me Grace."

Cat nodded to Nick, glanced at Emily, and gave them a quirk of her lip. Then Cat moved through the crowd toward the table with the food.

"Did you see the way she looked at me?" Emily asked.

Bryan sidled over to the table where Cat stood contemplating the food choices.

"How have you been?" Bryan asked.

Cat ignored him.

"Cat got your tongue?" Bryan asked, snickering.

She gave him a seething look.

"Guess not," Bryan said, edging away toward a group of guys from school.

Nick again felt rooted to the floor, his head in a turmoil of conflicting thoughts and feelings. *What if he started to have feelings for her? What if Emily didn't like them talking? What if...*

"I wish she would just stay away forever." Emily pouted.

"Nothing is going to happen." Nick massaged her shoulders. Even as he said those words, he could tell the problems were already starting.

Emily retorted, "Ha!"

"I need to talk to her about some things and our relationship—yours and mine. You're my girl and always will be." He winked.

Emily's face brightened somewhat as she fingered the intertwined hearts necklace. She sat by Gary and Tiffany. When Nick looked over at them, Emily was deep in conversation with Tiffany, but she kept fingering her necklace, and he was glad.

When the party drew to a close, Nick wished people "Happy New Year." While doing so, he kept one eye on Cat to ensure there were no problems with Emily.

Cat kept her distance and talked mainly with Nick's mother. Cat had eaten an enormous mountain of food, thanked his parents, and gave him a nod before leaving.

After all the people left, and the goodbyes and well-wishes said, Nick and Emily sat at the kitchen table, heads close together, talking.

"Nothing will change, I promise," Nick said, taking Emily's hand and squeezing it.

"Will she understand that?" Emily asked in an urgent whisper.

"She'll have to," Nick said.

"I don't think she'll give up easily. I know girls." Emily scowled.

"You're my girl."

Emily gave him a shaky smile. "We should have a plan."

"A plan?" Nick raised his eyebrow.

"What to do in class when she's around," Emily prompted.

"Ignore her?"

"I think we need to talk to her together," Emily said, folding her arms.

Nick didn't think that was a good idea and said, "You and me?" He swallowed back a painful lump in his throat.

What if Cat started talking about what had happened before? Being reincarnated? How was he to respond?

"Yes," Emily said, patting his arm. "We should do it together."

He nodded, feeling slightly nauseous.

Chapter 51

On Wednesday, when they returned to school, Cat re-enrolled. Again, she was the talk of the day—nothing else to be excited about on the gray, overcast winter's morning.

The whispers started almost immediately.

"Did you see what she's wearing?"

"What's she doing back?"

"She's so weird."

"I love her boots!"

On and on the comments went.

Nick heard the whispers as he and Emily found Cat at her locker. They clasped hands tightly—a unified front.

"Can we talk to you for a minute?" Nick asked.

Cat turned, her eyes moving up and down. "Let me guess—" She squinted. "—you're back together again?"

"Right," Nick said. *She knew that.* He had already told her.

"Congratulations," Cat said, although her comment was sarcastic.

That was it? No fight? Nothing?

"We just wanted you to understand." Emily brushed her burnt hand through her hair. She was intimidated by Cat's stature and stony expression.

"Oh, I do," she said with a knowing smile. "I do."

They turned to leave.

"It was nice seeing you at Del's," Cat said. "I've missed you...I mean, everyone." She moved her arms wide as if encompassing the whole school.

Emily's nails dug into his. She whipped back around. "When were you at Del's?" she demanded.

Nick shrugged. "The other day. I wanted to know about her 'help me' message."

"I bet!" Emily retorted. "Why did you send Nick that 'help me' message?" She took a step forward, making Cat back into her locker. "To try to win him back?"

"I don't need to do that," Cat said with a knowing smile.

"Like hell!" Emily hissed, her face turning red. "What did you want to talk to him about?"

"It can wait," Cat said.

Nick studied Emily's face—a mixture of loathing and disdain. A look he rarely saw on his "class-president-get-along-with-everyone" girlfriend.

Nick already had a sinking feeling in his stomach that being a solidified couple wouldn't make a difference. It was going to be difficult having Cat back at school.

Chapter 52

"Well, if it isn't Miss Catherine Thomlinson," Coach said when Cat came into the room with a slip from the office indicating she was back at school and returning to her classes.

Cat's eyes scanned the half-full classroom, resting on Nick in the back of the room. He realized he was holding his breath and let it out, waiting to see what would happen.

"Cat," she said, looking anything but pleased to be back at school in World History class again.

"Where did you go?" Coach asked, not taking note of the scorn on her face.

"Oregon." She started edging down the aisle.

Her terse reply ended Coach's questions. He waved to the desk next to Nick in the back of the room.

She took her seat and didn't look directly at him, instead staring straight ahead. Nick needed to change his seat so he wouldn't sit by her.

Coach began class by turning to the whiteboard and writing the dates of the Vietnamese conflict. Nick opened his notebook and started writing.

"I hope we can begin where we left off?" she whispered.

"No!" The word came out louder than he had expected, and all eyes turned to them. He lowered his voice. "I'm back with Emily and want to keep it that way."

"Nick? Catherine? Questions?" Coach asked.

"No questions from me!" Cat held up her hands.

"Nick?"

A million questions but nothing about World History or the Vietnam War. "Ditto."

"You'll change your mind," she said, smirking.

No, he wouldn't.

She settled back with a half-smile and folded her arms. "Later. You'll need me later."

Like hell he would. She looked like a satisfied cat with a slight smirk on her lips.

Cat hummed softly under her breath. Where had Nick heard that tune before? He wasn't sure. On autopilot he wrote down lecture notes.

When the bell sounded, Nick lingered after class, waiting to talk to Coach.

"Nick?" Coach leaned forward expectantly. "Can you start conditioning for football?"

"Uh, no. I mean, it's something else. Will you move my seat? I can't sit by Cat."

"Is there a problem?"

"Sort of. Cat doesn't like my girlfriend."

"Emily? How could anyone dislike her?" Coach looked surprised and lifted his brows before straightening a pile of papers on his desk and searching for his pen.

"I don't know; having her next to me makes it a bit more complicated. Do you know what I mean?"

"I do. You can sit in the front." He pointed toward a seat by the door.

"Thanks."

"Give some thought to conditioning."

"I will. I have, but I had a torn ligament fixed and am waiting for the all-clear."

Coach nodded, and Nick slipped out of the room.

* * * *

When the bell for lunch rang, Nick found Emily in the cafeteria. He ran his hands through his hair and shifted his feet.

"What's the matter?" Emily asked. She began unwrapping her sandwich.

"Em, I need to talk to Cat and get this straightened out." He jerked his chin to the corner where Cat sat by herself.

Her eyes narrowed. "Do you need me?"

"No, it's better if I talk to her alone."

Nick walked to where Cat sat. His steps slowed the closer he got. Cat sat by herself and appeared to be studying her phone.

"I thought you were ignoring me?" Cat said, raising her brows.

He smirked and placed his lunch tray on the table. Cat didn't have any food, only her cell phone.

"You want some French fries?"

Cat wrinkled her nose. "No, thanks."

Nick unwrapped his cheeseburger and opened his milk, readying his lunch for consumption. Cat watched him, remaining quiet and aloof.

"I need to share a couple of things," he said, taking a fry and dunking it in ketchup.

"Shoot."

He ate and swallowed before continuing, "Another person has been visiting me in my dreams, not Jean Claude."

She arched a brow. "I have multiple past lives,

too," she said.

"Well." He picked up his burger, taking a bite before adding, "I didn't know about others."

"So." She folded her arms and leaned back.

"I'm trying to get my life on track, and having you here isn't helping."

She reached over as if to take his hand but stopped. "Nick, we're supposed to be together."

"You're not part of this new alter."

Cat turned away and chuckled. "They've got you calling your past lives alters?"

"Yes, that's what the doctor called it. Alternative personalities."

"I remember many lives where we're together."

Nick swallowed. The effort caused a strangling feeling. He cleared his throat. "You never told me that."

"How could I? You didn't believe Jean Claude at first. How would you have responded if I told you we've had many lives together?"

Words seemed to have deserted him, and he stared at her with a slack jaw. He closed his mouth and pushed away his tray. His appetite had left him too. "I just want to be with Emily."

She shrugged. "You'll see, it's no use."

He struggled to his feet. "Let me worry about that!"

He could feel her eyes boring into the back of his head as he returned to Emily. He tossed the rest of his lunch in the garbage.

"Well?" Emily asked, giving him a sympathetic look. "How did she take it?" She tapped her sneakers with sequins that winked conspiratorially at him.

He moved his shoulders noncommittally.

"Will she leave us alone?" Emily asked, pushing up her glasses that slid down her nose.

He didn't think so, but he didn't want to tell Emily.

Nick's only response was to blow out his breath. He hoped Emily would think Cat agreed to leave him alone, but the opposite was true.

Chapter 53

I felt the life leave Emeline. She had been struggling and moaning, and then she was quiet—deathly quiet. I was familiar with death. I had lived with it daily during my time in the hospital tent. I hoped her last thoughts were of me holding her hand and whispering that I loved her.

I got out of bed, lit the lamp, and looked down at her peaceful face, turned slightly away from me like she was whispering something in my ear before she left. All I could see was her porcelain face—the burned parts under the quilt. She looked right beautiful to me.

I hobbled into the kitchen and lit the stove. It would be a long day as we prepared her to rest in the cemetery plot by her parents. I would need to keep my wits about me and comfort the girls as we prepared to say our goodbyes. I wouldn't just be burying Emeline, but the baby in her belly.

I put the coffee on to perk, and when finished, I took a cup, sat at the table, blackened from the fire, and waited to see day crack the horizon. The brew was bitter, and I longed for cream and sugar—still scarce. My shoulders slumped. How was I to keep the girls, tend the fields, and get around with one leg? Life sure was complicated sometimes.

Slowly the sun peeked over the horizon, and I could hear the girls stir from their beds. How was I to tell them their mama was dead? The mama who took loving care of them when I was gone?

Sophia was the first to descend the ladder from the loft. "Is Mama sleeping?"

"Yes."

Anne frowned at me. "How come she's not waking up?"

"She's sleeping," I repeated numbly.

Sophia approached the bed and fumbled for Emeline's hand. "She's cold, Daddy. Can't you tend the fire?"

"I could, but it's no use." I slumped back into the chair and opened my arms to them. "Your mama's gone to be with the Lord." I held them to me as long as I could. "I need you to run over to Uncle Garrett and Aunt Mildred's place and let them know about Mama and then go to the church and tell the preacher."

"And what will you do, Daddy?"

"Keep your mama company."

"Oh! Daddy!" They flung their arms around me and hugged me tight.

Chapter 54

The next day, Nick sat in his new seat when Cat entered World History. Her eyes stopped at Nick's desk near the door. She quirked a brow at him before taking her seat in the back of the room.

Coach began his lecture, and Nick felt himself tumbling and swirling away from the classroom to the Kentucky farm.

I bowed my head, clasped my hands, and prayed for Emeline's soul.

"Nick?" From far away, he heard a name and swiped at the tears on his cheeks.

But he continued to pray fervently.

"Nick!" Coach commanded. "Are you all right?"

"Lord…" Nick mumbled. "Take Em into your loving arms. She's a good woman."

He felt arms around him and smelled Cat's earthy-musk fragrance, but still, he couldn't get away from Jonathan.

"Who are you?" she whispered in his ear.

The question jolted him and almost made Jonathan disappear. "Jonathan." The rough coffin was blurry with tears of grief.

"Oh?" Her arms held him firmly. "And why is he crying?"

Nick sniffed. "My wife just died."

"Where are you?"

"Our farm in Kentucky."

"We're currently at Laketon High School." She gave his shoulders a little shake.

Nick sniffed and reached up to smooth away his tears. "I'm…"

"Hush," her soothing voice calmed him.

He looked up and around the room. The classroom was quiet, with everyone focusing on him. Several students had shocked expressions; even Bryan's typical smirk was gone.

Coach came over and put his hand on the desk. "Why don't you go to the office and call your parents to pick you up?"

"I'll go with him," Cat said.

"Thank you," Coach said.

Nick leaned against Cat, slowly got out of his seat, and followed her. Once in the hall, he stopped and slumped against the wall. "Oh, God, what's happening to me?" He moaned and scrubbed at his eyes with the heels of his palms.

"You're just having a moment," Cat said.

"It came on so suddenly. I don't know what to do." He sniffed, wiping his nose on his sleeve.

"I've got an idea—why don't I call Dr. Sims and see if she can help?"

"Do you think she can?" He blinked again, unseeing, as the gray lockers turned into soldiers before morphing back into lockers.

"I think maybe she can," Cat said. "Would you like me to call her?"

"Sure."

She offered her hand, and he took it and followed her from the school to her car. Once in the green Jag, she took out her phone and called, confirming Dr. Sims would see them today.

The Jag cut through the morning fog and swerved around slower drivers as they hurtled their way to Dr. Sim's office.

Nick's phone chimed with a text from his mother.

—*Coach called us. When are you coming home?*—

—*I'm with Cat.*—

—*Come home. We have an appointment with Dr. Patar.*—

He gulped, chewing briefly on his lower lip before turning off his phone and shoving it deep into his pocket.

Cat leaned over and frowned at him. "Who was that?"

"My mom. She has an appointment for me to see Dr. Patar." He noticed Cat's confused expression and added, "My therapist."

Cat nodded and tapped her fingers on the steering wheel. "She hasn't been able to help you."

Nick rubbed his face again and looked out the window at his red-rimmed eyes and blotchy cheeks in the side mirror. "I don't know what Dr. Sims can do either." He blew out a long breath.

Could anyone help him?

Chapter 55

They arrived at Dr. Sims' office. The dentist-office blandness of the waiting area hid the true nature of what the doctor did—past life regressions to help the living reconcile their past existences. She was waiting and beckoned them in.

Dr. Sims helped people remember their past lives by using relaxation to draw out visions/remembrances. Or was it the power of suggestion? This wasn't their first time seeing Dr. Sims. They had visited her when he believed he had been Jean Claude. Had Nick fantasized about these lives, and they were only dreams? And not actual occurrences? There was no time to figure that out now.

When they settled into her office, Dr. Sims said, "So tell me why you're here, Nick? Cat said it was an emergency."

He swallowed and moved his head. "I guess I lost it in class and couldn't get Jonathan out of my head."

Dr. Sims picked up the file on her desk and scanned the pages. "I don't remember anyone named Jonathan, only Jean Claude."

Nick licked his lips before answering. "Jonathan started coming to me after Jean Claude died."

"I see," she said, placing her hands on the file. "Can you tell me about Jonathan?"

His mind was relatively blank, but what did he

know of Jonathan? Another tortured soul like Jean Claude, only in different ways. "He's a soldier, he lost a leg in the war, and the army sent him home."

"And which war?" Dr. Sims asked.

"The Civil War, I think."

She didn't respond, so he continued, "His wife died."

His dreams were so vivid, but now, everything was black and white like the old pictures of long-lost relatives they had discovered in the garage. Involuntarily he reached down and massaged his left thigh—still there.

"What would you like me to do, Nick?" Dr. Sims asked.

"Make them go away."

"You know I can't do that, but sometimes knowledge has power. If you know Jonathan's real story, it might help you keep him at bay. Usually, past life remembrances leave in childhood, but yours have lingered. Perhaps there is trauma involved."

"I'm willing to try anything." He hung his head and studied the floor.

"Let's do a regression and see what comes of that."

Dr. Sims nodded toward Cat and the door, and before Nick could thank Cat for bringing him here, she left.

"Let's see what we can uncover about Jonathan. You ready?" Dr. Sims asked.

Nick settled himself on the couch and closed his eyes. "Yep. Relaxed. Long dark tunnel."

"Exactly. Let's get started." Even when he heard a rustle from Dr. Sims' desk, he kept his eyes closed and his breathing even and regular, relaxed.

"Envision your happy place."

There didn't seem to be happy places for him, but he forced himself to think of kissing Emily.

"Are you relaxed?"

"I think so."

"Your face looks tense."

Why wasn't he relaxed with Emily? He forced himself to go to the beach, a fantastic fall day with the waves frothy and white, the breeze ruffling his hair.

"Much better," she said. "Look for the tunnel."

He saw the long dark tunnel and eagerly stepped into it, knowing he'd eventually find the bright light at the end and see Jonathan again.

"I'm in."

"Walk toward the light."

Momentarily, the light blinded him. After a moment, he opened them. His eyes swept the room, finally resting on a woman working the dough on a scarred table, her hands covered with flour, a cat hidden in the shadows of the doorway, and a lantern lighting the woman's work surface.

"What do you see?"

"A woman is making bread."

"Do you know where you are?"

"A kitchen. Not modern, but old-fashioned."

"Anything else?"

"A kerosene lantern."

"Is that the only light?"

Nick scanned the room again. The single window let in a glimpse of the moon. "No, it's nighttime, and the moon's shining."

"Do you know this woman?"

He knew her. A tallish woman with a stern face,

square jaw, and small eyes, her hair in a bun at the back of her head. "Her name is Emeline." He was sure of it. "Jonathan's wife. I...I remember her."

"Is she a nice person?"

"I think she is. She's tired. Her belly's rounded. She's going to have a baby."

"I see." Dr. Sims' voice got softer. "What else?"

"A cat jumped onto the table where she's working, and she tried to hit it away and knocked over the lamp instead."

Nick watched as kerosene crackled with fire and raced toward the dough and the sleeve of Emeline's dress. Like a passerby to an accident, he watched the flame eat up her sleeve and catch on her hair, all in slow motion. He tried to wrestle out of the stranglehold he felt as he watched so he could go to her, but he was powerless to move.

Emeline screamed, "Help! Help me! Please!"

Nick flinched at the high-pitched sounds coming from the burning woman. He watched as Jonathan entered the kitchen with his crutches and saw his wife ablaze.

Thank goodness! Help for the poor woman!

"Help me!" Emeline sobs.

She shrieks and flings herself back and forth, tearing at her clothing, trying to escape the flames.

Jonathan knocks her to the floor. "Roll around!" He had seen men on fire roll in the dirt. There was no dirt on the floor, and his wife twisted herself back and forth, leaving half of her black like a log on the fire too long. Finally, she lay on the floor in a heap, writhing and groaning.

"What happened?" Nick hears Jonathan ask.

"The cat!"

"The cat?"

Jonathan scratched his chin. The itty-bitty Stormy? She couldn't have set her on fire! Preposterous! The kerosene lamp was large, and he didn't think the cat was capable of such carnage.

Nick shook his head. "The cat!" he mumbled. "It was the cat!"

"Can we move forward in time?" Dr. Sims prompted. "What do you see?"

Nick saw Jonathan by a mound of dirt, and his head bowed, praying. "He's praying and sad."

"What's he sad about?"

"His wife. Emeline has died."

"How?"

"She never healed from the fire. She blamed it on the cat. It was she who knocked over the lantern."

"Who do you think the wife is?"

"I don't know."

"Could she be Cat?"

"I don't know." The gray cat was sitting nearby, watching Jonathan, waiting for him.

Nick willed himself to stay when he felt his body float away from Jonathan toward the tunnel, but he wasn't strong enough to resist. "I'm going back to the tunnel," he told Dr. Sims.

****

Nick returned to himself slowly, the fog clearing from the air, first a blur, then an outline, one or two limbs, and finally his whole being.

He opened his eyes and concentrated on Dr. Sims' ceiling as he tried to make sense of what he had seen of his former self. Was he Jonathan? What was Jonathan's last name? If he knew, he could try to look him up.

Dr. Sims sat quietly, waiting for him to speak.

"Not what I expected," he said.

"No?"

"I wanted to learn more about Jonathan. Not his wife." Nick shook his head and examined all the bits and pieces he knew of Jonathan so far. Perhaps Cat wasn't part of this past life? He reverently wished she wasn't, even though she might be. "I don't think Cat was there, unlike before when she was Chaton."

"What makes you think that?"

Nick was quiet.

"Most people don't reacquaint in each life," Dr. Sims said. "But some do," she added.

So he'd been with Cat forever? But he wanted Emily!

Something popped into his head, and his jaw dropped.

Dr. Sims leaned forward, and expectation made her brows raise.

"I think…" He massaged his temples. "She told me once…" Then he moved his shoulders as if they pained him. "She was a cat."

"Interesting."

"Can people be reincarnated as animals?"

"I don't know. It would be a first for me."

When they finished, Cat led Nick away from Dr. Sims' office and to her car. She was quiet and didn't say anything. Nick sat in his seat with his hands limply hanging down. He didn't fasten his seat belt, and Cat didn't turn on the car.

"You're quiet," she said as she fastened her seat belt.

Nick did the same and seemed to have found his voice. "Wondering what it all means and how to make it stop." He kept his gaze out the window. "How did you get past Chaton?"

"I haven't," Cat said, "but I understand her better."

"How does knowing about Jonathan stop me from thinking and acting like him?"

Cat was quiet for a long while. The green mile markers continued to whip past as she drove.

"The past life regressionist I saw in Oregon said Chaton revealed herself when there was trauma in my life. I knew of her when I was a little girl."

Nick straightened and turned toward Cat. "What sort of trauma?"

She shrugged but continued to watch the road ahead. The only indication she was tense was her fingers clenching the steering wheel. "Not knowing my real family."

"But your brother…"

"He's a snake in the grass," she said, shaking her head. "I'm not sure he is my biological brother." She paused and adjusted her rearview mirror. "A few of the Romas I met were evil people!"

"But what about you?"

"I don't think I'm a bad person who wants to cheat people to make money."

Nick gave a single nod. Cat drove a Jag and had nice clothing. She didn't need to lie and steal.

He finally responded, "That's got to be hard knowing bad things about your family." Nick absently rubbed at his left knee. "I don't think I have anything like that in my family."

She looked toward him briefly but remained quiet.

What sort of trauma could make him remember all these other people? Was it a concussion from falling from the tree or being tackled in football? He was sure he wasn't adopted. The family resemblance was apparent between Nick and his parents. A concussion would be the answer for the time being.

Chapter 56

"Nick! Where have you been?" His parents were waiting by the door when he came in; their faces furrowed with concern. Cat had dropped him off and driven away.

"I just needed to clear my head."

"You missed an appointment with Dr. Patar." His mother glanced at her watch and screwed up her face.

"I'm sorry. I wasn't thinking straight."

"Let me call Dr. Patar and let her know you're home safe."

Nick sank into a chair and fingered his phone and the missed calls. Emily had called multiple times.

He blew out his breath and called her.

"Nick!" she practically shouted, answering. "Everyone was worried about you! Your parents called me."

"Why?"

"Your mother wanted to know if you were with me, and I told her no. Where were you?"

"Thinking."

Nick thought he heard her inhale.

"Oh?"

"I was at the beach," he lied. No use getting Emily all riled about him being with Cat.

"Are you okay now?" she asked.

He blew out his breath. "I'm seeing the

psychologist soon, and maybe she can give me something." But he remembered her telling him there wasn't a magic pill for DID.

"Oh, gosh, Nick! What can I do?" Emily asked, her voice rising into a squeak.

"Nothing. I think this is something I have to overcome myself." Did he suppose that was even possible with what he knew?

The shaking he had felt in the class started deep in his belly and continued outward, making his teeth chatter, and the feeling of dread enveloped him.

"I better go," he said briefly through clenched teeth.

"Nick!" Emily said.

He turned off the phone as his mother fussed over him, wrapping him in a wool blanket. He continued crawling deep into himself, where it was dark, and demons lurked. Even wrapped in a blanket, he shook as the demons circled—waiting.

****

After a sleepless night, Nick slunk into Dr. Patar's office and waited for his appointment. He had spent the night avoiding sleep so he wouldn't need to see Jonathan. The mirror reflected his ordeal—dark circles, red-rimmed eyes, and a haggard slack jaw. No, he hadn't thought about Jonathan, only about the black fingers of sleep that needled him as he drank coffee and walked around his bedroom, periodically slapping his cheeks to keep his eyes open.

Dr. Patar smiled warmly, and Nick straightened and tried to smile back, but the sleeplessness weighed on him and made him want to sink into a puddle. If he opened his mouth, his teeth chattered together.

"Your parents called me and said you had an episode at school yesterday." Dr. Patar launched into their session—no pleasantries today.

Nick's brain grappled with the word episode—a general catch-all term including a breakdown and mental disorders—he remembered. The quivers started in his stomach, and he pushed Jonathan aside.

"I don't remember much." He stopped talking and closed his mouth to keep his teeth from clicking together, then continued, "Except that I couldn't get away from Jonathan." Even now, his mind swirled with black smoke.

"Your alter?"

"Yes." His teeth continued to clank together.

"What do you think brought that on?"

"Cat."

Dr. Patar frowned as if she couldn't remember who Cat was.

Nick prompted her. "She's the girl—" He stopped and closed his mouth again until his teeth stopped clicking together. "—who said we were reincarnated."

"Ah, yes! The Gypsy girl?" Dr. Patar folded her hands on the desk and leaned forward slightly. "Anything else been happening besides seeing Cat?"

"Not really. Things were starting to return to normal." And he wished the shaking would stop.

"Define 'normal' for me?" she asked.

Nick leaned back and studied the ceiling. "Normal is—" He blew out his breath and moved his jaw around to loosen it. "—normal is good grades, being with my girlfriend, and following my Christian faith."

"That sounds like a good life to me."

Should he tell her about Dr. Sims?

"There is one other thing I want to add." Mercifully his teeth stopped chattering, and Dr. Patar remained quiet but lifted her brows. "I missed my appointment yesterday because I went to see a woman who does past-life regressions."

"I'm not familiar with what that entails. Can you explain?"

He'd try.

"She uses relaxation to help me remember my past life. So far, I have two lives."

"It sounds similar to what I was going to suggest."

"Really?"

"Yes, hypnosis to examine the trauma causing these alters to come out."

"Will I remember Jonathan again?"

"I'm not sure what will come of hypnosis for you. I want to know what trauma may be triggering Jonathan to appear."

Nick looked around her office. She didn't have a couch like Dr. Sims, only two chairs to sit on. "Do you...do you do it here?"

"No, I'm going to suggest a hypnotherapist." Dr. Patar paused and picked up her notepad. "If it's okay, I'd like your parents to come in while I explain what I'm proposing you do, and if they agree, give you a referral to see a therapist."

Nick nodded, and soon his parents came into the office. His mother sat next to him, and his father stood and put his hands on Nick's shoulders.

"As I told Nick," Dr. Patar began, "I'd like to refer him to a hypnotherapist and see if he can remember the stress or trauma causing alternate personalities to reveal themselves at this point."

"Hypnosis?" his mother said before reaching over and grasping Nick's hand. His father's touch tightened on his shoulders.

His father cleared his throat. "I understand hypnosis can put suggestions into a person's brain." Nick turned to look up at his father.

His father's gaze dropped to the floor before he added, "The medical community doesn't sanction it."

Why the hesitation? The parents had him exorcised when he was a kid because he talked about Jean Claude and being a WWII soldier!

"I've used it before with about seventy-five percent accuracy. And it was able to help my clients pinpoint when the trauma started. Or even remember the trauma," Dr. Patar continued.

"I see," his father said. "I guess I'm willing to do anything to help Nick."

"Me too," his mother said.

They were quiet on their way home. Nick sat in the backseat and looked unseeing out the window. His phone buzzed in his pocket, but he ignored it.

"Does anyone want a burger and fries?" Nick's dad asked.

His mother shook her head.

"Nick?"

"No, I'm not hungry."

"Okay…" His father looked back at him from the rearview mirror. "That's a first."

Nick forced a smile, but the effort made his teeth chatter, so he shrugged and continued looking out the window.

Chapter 57

Emily continued texting him until they pulled into their driveway. When Nick returned to his bedroom, he looked at his phone and answered her messages.

—*How was your appt?*—

—*OK.*—

—*Did you get meds?*—

There was no medicine for what ailed him. It was as if someone had put a damp wool blanket over him, and he couldn't get away, smothering him.

—*No.*—

—*Will you be at school tomorrow?*—

—*IDK.*—

—*Let me know if I can help.*—

He sent her a happy face emoji.

He stowed his phone and lay on his bed, first on his back, staring at the ceiling, then rolling over to his side and curling into a fetal position. Nick held tightly to his knees, hoping the pressure would stop the internal chills. He didn't know how long he lay there, but the darkness outlined the window, and he heard footsteps on the stairs. He couldn't reach his phone, but he thought it was late.

"Nick? Are you doing okay?" his mother asked.

No, he was still shaking, his insides jarring against each other.

His mother came in, pulled up the comforter over

him, and smoothed back his hair. "Are you cold?"

An internal frost.

"I don't know."

"You're shaking."

"I guess I am."

"I'll call the hypnotherapist tomorrow and get you an appointment."

He nodded, and when he didn't respond further, she bent down and kissed his forehead and said, "We love you, son," before closing the door softly behind her.

He was alone, yet, he wasn't.

****

The hypnotherapist, Dr. Frowd, looked a bit like the devil with a pointed black beard and jet colored hair, and penetrating green eyes. Nick swallowed when he entered the office. The shakes still rattled him, and he felt slightly nauseous at Jonathan's intrusion into his life.

"Hello, Nick. I'm Dr. Frowd." He extended his hand, but Nick didn't shake it.

Did he say Freud?

Nick blinked and moved his chin down.

Dr. Frowd paused and appeared to be waiting for him to say more.

Finally, the doctor cleared his throat and said, "I conferred with Dr. Patar at length after she spoke to you and your parents."

Nick watched as the doctor talked.

"She seems to think you've had some trauma from your past. Do you remember anything?"

"I fell."

"She mentioned you fell out of a tree, played

football, and suffered a concussion at one point."

When Nick stayed mute, the doctor continued, "Have you witnessed an accident or something else that might make an alter show themselves?"

"I dunno."

"She suggested hypnosis. Would you be okay with that?"

Nick nodded again.

"Hypnosis isn't a scary thing. I'll use imagery and suggestions to relax you before asking you to sort through memories and see if we can pinpoint how you were traumatized."

Hypnosis was almost the same as a past-life regression. *Maybe Frowd and Sims should get together and share notes.*

When he was relaxed, a scene unfolded before him. Elementary-age Nick burst into the house, clenching a paper to share with his grandparents. "Grammy! Grampy!"

The house was quiet and seemed empty, but the door was unlocked. Would his grandparents leave and not lock the door?

"Where are you, Nick?" Dr. Frowd asked.

"I…I…" Nick couldn't finish the thought.

He paused in the hallway and listened. From far away, he heard the undercurrent of voices. His grandparents hadn't heard him. They were at the back of the house. Nick called again, but still, there was no cheery greeting of "Hi, Nicky! How was your day?"

The voices were coming from the television in his grandfather's den. No one was watching the TV, but the side table was covered with empty medicine bottles. Nick saw some black shoes sticking out from next to the couch. He backed up and held his breath.

"Grandpa? Is that you?"

There was no answer. He crept forward. Now he saw pant legs, his grandfather's belt (the one with U.S. Army Proud stamped into the buckle), and Grandpa's face. It looked like Grandpa, but yet it didn't. Grandpa's eyes were open and staring. With a tentative finger, Nick reached out to touch the claw-like hand. Grandpa was cold, and Nick felt his stomach push into a ball as he whirled and ran from the room. "Grandma! Something's the matter with Grandpa!"

Nick ran from his grandparents' house and tore across the street for home, where a car barely missed him. The honking followed Nick into the house, to his bedroom, where he hid under the bed and waited for Grandpa to wake up. And then everything went black.

"Nick, what did you see?" Dr. Frowd asked.

Nick continued to shake and blacked out until he smelled something nasty and sharp under his nose— smelling salts. And then his parents' concerned voices asked if he was all right. His father helped him stand and eased him into a chair.

"You reacted to the hypnosis," his mother said, her hands cool on his feverish face.

Nick nodded. The pieces of what he saw were disjointed and out of order—something about shoes.

"Did you see something that upset you?" his father asked.

He thought he had, but everything was blacked out.

"I think Nick should be checked into Westview Hospital for evaluation," Dr. Frowd said.

"What's that?" his mother asked.

"It's the mental health hospital," Dr. Frowd

explained. "I think Nick remembered something that triggered his reaction."

"Nick, can you tell us what upset you?" his father asked.

"No!" He folded his arms, ducked his chin to his chest, and slumped down in the chair.

"Would you like me to confer with Dr. Patar?" Dr. Frowd asked.

"It's just so sudden. We thought he'd be hypnotized, and then we could go home," his mother said, concern laced in her voice.

Nick shook and clenched his teeth together so he wouldn't bite his tongue.

"Nick?" his father asked. "We're going to take you to the hospital for evaluation. Will that be okay with you?"

Nick shook his head up and down and back and forth.

"Okay, let's go," his father said, taking his hand and helping him from the chair and then to the car.

Chapter 58

Nick awoke and blinked at the unfamiliar ceiling. He wasn't sure where he was or what had happened. Nick tried moving his arm, even jerking at it with all his strength, but it remained at his side. He tilted his head and saw the straps around his wrists. Why was he strapped to the bed in a white, stainless-steel room? It looked and smelled like the hospital. He wrinkled his nose at the smell of bleach, an undertone of urine, and something metallic and medicinal. How in the heck had he gotten here?

The last thing he remembered was getting a shot in the arm—and when he awoke, he was here, fastened to a bed. There had to be some mistake. Flexing his arm, he pulled against the restraint—there was no give.

He had been talking to that doctor—the weird and kind of evil-looking guy. Nick couldn't remember his name, and then he was here. Where were his parents? Did they know he was here?

He could move his head, saw a red button near his right hand, and pressed it. Nothing happened, no lights, or sirens, nothing. But soon, the door handle jiggled, and a nurse came in wearing blue scrubs and a pasted-on smile.

"And how are you today, Nicholas?" Her voice rose as if she might break into a song.

"I want to know what's going on," he demanded.

"I'll let the doctor on call know you're awake," she said.

"Can I use the bathroom?"

"Not until the doctor says it's okay."

"So, I'm supposed to piss myself?"

She gave him another forced smile. "You have a catheter."

Oh, God! This situation kept getting worse and worse!

She checked the IV in his left hand and looked at the bags of clear fluids dripping into his body. If he clenched his left hand, he felt the needle sting in the vein.

"I want to see my parents."

She nodded but didn't respond.

****

Nick floated in and out of consciousness. It was hard to tell what day it was—a shade was covering the window. The light from the hallway was bright, but it was always shining. Several machines had lights that glowed on the whiteboard with his name printed in neat black letters and the nurses' and CNAs' names.

The next time he awoke, his parents sat on each side of the bed. "Boy, am I glad to see you! What's going on?" He pulled against the straps.

Nick turned his head toward his father, who licked his lips. "You had a reaction at the hypnotherapist's office."

"What kind of reaction?" Nick frowned, trying to search his recent memories for what had happened.

"You threw up and tried to take a swing at your father," his mother said quietly. Her eyes were shiny and tear-filled.

"Gosh!" Nick's eyes widened. "I'm sorry."

His father reached out to stroke his cheek. "It's okay, son."

"I'd like to go home." Nick turned to his mom. "I'll make it up to you guys at home."

"Dr. Patar and the on-call doctor will need to confer and see if you're safe to go home."

"What about school?"

His mother moved her shoulders. "It'll have to wait until you're better."

"Have you talked to Emily?"

"Yes, she's worried too," his mother said.

"Can she visit? How about Gary?"

His mother shook her head vehemently. "No, only family at this point."

"Can't you say she's my cousin?"

"No," his father said firmly. "We'll play by the rules."

It didn't seem fair. It was his life—couldn't he make up the rules?

Chapter 59

"Please, Daddy, can't Stormy come into the house?" Sophia cried, her face red from sobbing for her mother, now resting in the family plot with a small wooden cross with her name on it, the only adornment.

"Let me think on it. I've never had a pet. Most of the animals here have a job to do. The cats take care of the mice by the corn."

Sophia sniffed. *"I don't know why! She's just an itty bitty kitty!"*

I patted her head. *"I know. I know."* I turned and swung out of the barn into the cold and wrapped my coat snugly around me. The girls needed something to hold on to with Emeline gone. My resolve to keep the cat in the barn was slipping.

Later, Stormy slept between Anne and Sophia, and I heard Sophia say, *"Please go to Daddy. He's lonely too."*

Chapter 60

Nick awoke again. The furniture, what little there was, came into focus—a table, two chairs, a cupboard, a sink, and a toilet. His life consisted of awake and sleeping moments. He was still in a hospital. And why he came to that conclusion, he wasn't sure. The smells—that was it—hospitals smelled strongly of bleach, blood, and other unsavory scents. He didn't have long to consider why he was there when the knob jiggled on the door. Nick tried to sit, but he was still restrained and craned his neck to see who was entering.

"Nick? It's Dr. Patar. Are you able to talk to me?" She wore a badge that listed her name and Westview Hospital. He wasn't familiar with Westview.

Nick? An unfamiliar name. He liked the name Nick. Nicolas of the Bible, a disciple ordained by the apostles?

"I can talk." Was he being interrogated? Could this be considered collaborating with the enemy?

"Can you tell me what happened? I've spoken to your parents, and they said you have been saying some unusual things."

"We were ambushed." *I shuddered, recalling the blue against gray bodies, the screams and shrieks, and the whizzing of bullets—one taking a bite out of my leg.*

"Ambushed? How do you mean?"

"We fought the best we could. The Rebs were

ruthless. Cabin Creek."

My nostrils flared as I recalled the scene—the dead/dying, the tang of freshly let blood, vomit, and defecation. Worse than any pigsty.

"Oh," she said in surprise. "You're Jonathan. Can you tell me more?"

More? This woman wanted more destruction and carnage? I was focusing on getting my crop in with one leg! Sophia and Anne had been helping the best they could, and the neighbor's borrowed mule was also helping, but it was as old as Methuselah from the good book.

Dr. Patar continued speaking. He knew she was a doctor, not a sawbones. She was a talker, not a doer. *I normally don't like chatty women, but this one would have to do with Emeline gone.* "You were talking about losing your leg."

"The Rebs shot me, and Sawbones took my leg. The gangrene."

"I see." She stood. "Maybe you should get some sleep?"

"Do you think I'll grow another leg?"

That shut her up!

****

When he awoke, Dr. Patar was still there, sitting by the bed, notebook and pen in hand.

"Nick?"

"Hmm." The pieces of his life came together, and he was whole.

"Are you Nick?"

"Who…" He wanted to rub the sleep from his eyes, but his arms and hands didn't move, tethered to the bed. He tried sitting up. "Why did you ask who I was?"

"Your alternate personalities have presented themselves."

He had had vivid dreams of Jonathan and Emeline.

"Is the cat still here?"

"You mean Cat?" Dr. Patar asked, clearly confused.

She was quiet, and Nick heard rustling pages.

"What triggered Jonathan to come out again?" Dr. Patar asked.

"What do you mean?"

"What triggered those other personalities to come out of hiding?"

How was he to know? He wasn't the doctor, after all.

"Dunno."

****

Later, after the doctor had left, Nick slept, or rather, he was enveloped in a black, drug-induced fog and state of being, suspended in his head, void of thoughts and feelings. He knew it was from drugs by the taste of medicine in the far back of his mouth. Even swallowing over and over didn't remove the taste. He remained in this other world. At least he wasn't bedeviled by the alters.

He was trapped and alone until the door opened softly and stealthily. He turned his head toward the sound. Cat. It took a few moments to register she was in his room. She had abandoned her customary black and was wearing blue hospital scrubs.

"I'm not supposed to have visitors," he said, lifting his head off the pillow.

"I'm here to change your sheets," she said.

"Pretty hard to do since I'm in bed," he said, trying

to be funny in an unhumorous situation.

"I just wanted to see you." She came to his side, her eyes unfathomable. He couldn't read what she was thinking.

He closed his eyes and blew out his breath. He'd rather have seen Emily, but Cat was here. Things were complicated when he was involved with her. He heard her feet shift, and she remained standing by his bed. He closed his eyes tighter.

"I can never stay away from you, Nick. You need to remember."

"I know." And on some intrinsic level, he did. It was easier with Emily, but who promised life would be easy? If he remembered his father's Bible teachings, very few Biblical people had it easy.

"We always help each other. Don't you remember?" she prompted.

He didn't remember. Why the pull between them? He knew they were wrong together, but still, he wanted Cat. And he wanted Emily too. As his mother was fond of saying, "he couldn't have his cake and eat it too." Nick was Judas of the Bible. Judas had betrayed Jesus. Now Nick was denouncing Emily—the sin was evil and all-consuming.

His nose itched now, and he felt her body taking up some of the space around him. He didn't need to open his eyes. He knew and felt her presence in his being.

"Can you scratch my nose?"

She did.

"Help me get out of here." Emily would never do anything as daring as sneak into the hospital.

"I'll bring you some scrubs tomorrow. You'll blend in with the rest of the staff."

His eyes popped open, taking in the sparse, impersonal room.

"I just want to get out of this bed and scratch my nose."

She began unfastening the strap, holding his arm down. Fumbling and cursing. "Shit!" She was nervous.

When his arm was free, he reached up and rubbed his nose, hoping he would be anyplace other than the hospital when he opened his eyes again.

He closed them and willed the hospital to disappear. Nope—he was still here—when he opened them, the room was complete with overhead fluorescent lighting and in a bed with side rails.

"I need to refasten your bonds." She took his wrist and gently put it back in the strap. Electricity ran up and down, raising the hair on his arms.

"You'll come tomorrow?" he asked, suddenly not wanting her to go.

"Yes," she promised and began humming a wordless tune as she left.

Chapter 61

"Help! Help! Where am I?" Nick awoke from another black, drug-induced sleep.

A face appeared in the small square window, and then he heard the door click, and a man came in.

"How are you feeling today, Nicholas?"

"My name's Jonathan."

"Ahh. I see. How is Jonathan feeling today?" Nick frowned at the man who was keeping his face neutral and calm.

"I'd like to get out of here."

"It's time for your medication." The man's words were soothing and low.

"I just need a shot of whiskey." The man wore a blue uniform, not Yankee blue, a lighter blue, which he favored on Emeline.

"This is better than whiskey. You'll feel calm and relaxed."

"No, I need to be on guard. Don't you see them?" In Nick's peripheral vision, he saw the gray-huddled mass of Rebel soldiers.

"Who?" The man's head swung around the room in a cursory fashion.

"The Rebels. They're hiding in the trees." Since he couldn't move his hands, he lifted a finger. "Behind you. Look. Don't you see them?"

The man turned. "Only a cupboard and sink."

"No! They're in the trees hiding!"

"Here, take this." The man in the blue uniform tipped a small pill into Nick's mouth and gave him a sip of water. "Have you swallowed it?"

Would it help? A pill was a funny thing to take for pain. He wasn't a sawbones, after all, just a soldier trying to survive.

****

Nick awoke to see his parents sitting by his hospital bed, his mother's head bowed, reading the Bible. For once, his head was clear and free from confusion.

"M-Mom?" he asked.

"Hi." Her eyes brightened as she leaned toward him.

"How long have I been here?" Nick's nose twitched, and he felt a sneeze coming on.

"You've been delirious."

All he could remember was something about a cat.

"Do we have a cat?"

His mother arched her brows. "Yes. Minnie?"

Minnie didn't sound right, but he was in a hospital and couldn't remember why.

He wrinkled his nose again, a sneeze making it itch. "Can you scratch my nose?"

She stood, placed the Bible on the chair, and gently rubbed his nose. "Better?"

He nodded. "Can you unfasten the straps?"

His mother looked toward the door with the small window that led to the hallway. She turned back to him and unfastened his right hand.

Nick studied it as he flexed it open and closed. He turned it over and frowned at the smooth palms.

Shouldn't they be work-worn and callused?

When he drifted off, he awoke to his parents' concerned faces hovering over him again. They were wearing different clothes, he thought.

"Are you still here?" Nick asked.

"We just returned," his father said.

"How are you doing, son?" his mother asked, smoothing back his hair from his forehead, her fingers cool on his skin.

"Better."

"You had us worried," his father said, using his palms to wipe his face in relief.

"That bad?" The words came automatically.

"Extremely. You were confused and sick. We've been praying. The congregation has formed a prayer chain," his father said.

Nick gave him a small smile.

"Prayers have been answered."

Nick nodded. "I feel like crap." He lifted his left hand—the restraints were gone! He didn't remember anyone taking them off. Now, his hand had an IV taped to it, and a bag of clear fluid swung near his head.

His mother laughed. "I'd say you were feeling better."

"Thanks for bringing Minnie to visit."

"I think you dreamed that," his father said.

"I remember Minnie sitting by me."

"We didn't bring Minnie," his father said. "No pets allowed."

He could have sworn he had petted her. She gave him comfort after surgery. She was sitting on his chest, cleaning herself. Fastidious, as always.

On their next visit, his mother kissed his cheek

before saying his name. "Nick!" His hospitalization had to be hard on them too.

"We can only stay for a short while." His mother kept looking toward the door where a man in scrubs waited. "The weather is horrible, and the roads are slippery."

"I'm glad you came," Nick said. "When can I get out of here?"

"When they think you're ready." His dad gave him a tight smile.

"I am."

"Unfortunately, you don't have much of a say." His mom scrunched her face. "They don't want you to hurt yourself."

"Hey—" Nick thought. "—how long have I been here?"

"A little over a week," his mom replied.

"You're not missing much," his dad added. "School has been called off for most of the week." His dad rubbed his hands together. "It's storming and blowing out there." He motioned with his chin. "We're in for some more bad weather."

The shades were closed. Nick couldn't see outside.

"Would you like to see?" his mother asked.

"Sure." He didn't care one way or another.

"Stormy weather," his father said, raising the shades so Nick could see white that stretched to the horizon.

Stormy weather. That rang a bell, but he couldn't remember why.

Chapter 62

True to her word, Cat returned, dressed in hospital scrubs, carrying a covered tray. Although Nick couldn't remember when that was—two days? Four? He had lost track.

"Sorry I couldn't get back before, but we're having a huge blizzard, and we were snowed in."

He frowned. "Stormy weather?" He moved his chin toward the covered tray. "Lunch?" Nick hoped it was anything other than hospital food.

She laughed as she pulled off the cover, revealing another set of hospital scrubs and a battered pair of sneakers that looked too big. "Lunch is served!"

"Am I glad to see you." He sobered. "Why? Why are you here?"

"What?" She gave him an innocent look and a slight shrug.

"Why are you doing this for me?"

"Silly question." She chuckled softly. "We've been helping each other out since our souls were created." She unfolded the scrubs and placed them on the bed.

Nick didn't respond. Had they been together in all past lives or just a few? How was Cat connected to Jonathan? Was she the cat in his dreams? After all, she said she was a cat once.

"You could be in big trouble. We both could," Nick said.

"I don't care. All I want is you." She folded her arms.

And he cared about Emily. She was better for him than Cat.

"Cat…what about Emily?"

Cat's face turned stony.

Nick slumped against the bed. "She won't understand if we're friends."

"And she'll never understand," Cat said, putting her fists on her hips.

"I need to try. Explain we're just friends."

"Just friends?" Cat's brows rose. "She won't believe you." Cat sauntered, surveying the room, her gaze stopping on the closet. "Most people don't remember their past lives." Her words were muffled as she looked through the closet.

"Does everyone have past lives?" he asked.

"No." She turned from her perusal of the closet.

"What do you suppose will happen when they find I'm gone?" Nick asked, struggling upright. His head swam and wavered after lying down for so long. He took in a ragged breath and steadied his racing heart. He picked off the tape holding the IV in place. He sucked in his breath and pulled the needle out, leaving a pimple of blood. "Dang! That hurt!"

"I imagine they'll send the police or security," Cat said, turning to the cupboards and searching the boxes and then handing him a bandage.

"It's too bad we didn't have something to put in the bed." Nick peered around the room for a person-sized dummy or blow-up doll. No such items in his room.

He stretched, feeling the joints of his back pop. He walked around slowly, letting the circulation return to his legs and feet.

Cat sat on the edge of the bed and watched. "You know, you'll come back to me."

He stopped his walking and faced her. "I'm happier when you're not here. That sounds mean, but my life was almost normal until you returned."

"So what are you saying?"

"We may—" He did air quotes with his fingers. "—have been together before or not. But I'm not sure it was a good thing."

"And do you believe that?"

"I'm not sure what I believe. The psychologist thinks I have a personality disorder."

She folded her arms and leaned against the pillows on the bed.

"It's more plausible than being reincarnated repeatedly." He grasped the railing on the bed, his knuckles turning white.

"Why is having a regenerated soul so terrible?" she asked, leaning back and using her arms for support.

"Reincarnation sounds so sci-fi and spooky."

"I see—" Cat pouted. "—so you don't believe we were together before? What about when your parents had you exorcised? I bet they believed it then!"

"Until you appeared in my life, I could push the other personalities aside. Now they're overtaking me, running my life. I need to get back to normal, Cat. I can do that better if you're not around."

"You're wrong. We need to be together as a couple. Only then will you have a chance at a normal life."

Nick moved his shoulders around as he contemplated her words.

"This is affecting my life too!" Cat said.

Nick heard voices outside his door. They both stopped to listen, and when the voices faded, she said, "We gotta get out of here." She handed him the scrubs.

Nick changed while she watched, biting her lip at his nakedness. He couldn't read her facial expression except her pursed mouth as if she longed for him. He slipped on the scrubs, and she stowed his hospital gown in the closet. He tried on the sneakers, but they were too big. "Can you hand me my sneakers in the closet? These things are waaay too big."

When dressed, she surveyed him. "You look like you work here."

He rubbed his chin. He hadn't shaved in a couple of weeks. If he worked here, he was one scruffy, smelly, messy-haired employee.

Would they be able to pull this off?

He glanced toward the window, but the snow swirling outside obscured everything.

"Let's arrange the bed, so it looks like someone is sleeping under the covers," he suggested.

They bunched up the blankets to make a lumpy outline. When finished, Cat went to the door and peered out. She motioned for him to follow. He picked up the tray, so it looked like he was bringing something to a patient on the floor. No one seemed to pay any attention to them. Nick nodded to one nurse who glanced their way briefly before ducking into a room.

They left through the fire exit stairs.

The wind and snow hit them as soon as they opened the double doors to the parking lot. They both wore hospital scrubs, lightweight with short sleeves. All the cars were lumpy bumps under piles of snow.

"I bet my car's buried," Cat said, chewing on her bottom lip in agitation and concern.

"Do you think we'll even get out of the lot?" Nick asked.

"Let's try!" They ran through the snow toward the mound that was Cat's green Jag, her license plate the only part that showed. Neither had any protection from the pelting sleet. With some difficulty, they brushed away snow and opened the door. Nick's hands were on fire from the cold—a strange sensation. They got into the Jag, and Cat turned on the heater. They would have to wait out the storm.

They got into the backseat. Cat put her arms around him, and he, her. The heater kicked on, and the inside already felt warmer.

The storm continued to rage around them, the wind rocking the car. Nick looked out the side window, starting to defrost. He wasn't sure how fast the snow was descending. At this rate, they would be covered and trapped.

He was so close to Cat several strands of her hair tickled his nose. She smelled of something earthy and sweet when she leaned into him. The curve of her body fit with his. He wanted to kiss her—a powerful urge he couldn't shake.

His feelings were hard to reconcile. He wanted Emily's steadying influence in his life, yet he lusted after Cat. It wasn't something he could control. He wanted both of them.

His feelings for Emily felt different. They connected because of their popularity and shared values. Cat affected him on many levels—spiritual, emotional, and primal. He wanted to kiss her. Kiss her like before.

He tightened his arms around Cat. She turned so they were chest to chest and put her head in the curve of his shoulder and neck. He liked having her close. Her presence was so different than Emily's.

They kissed. Cat's lips opened slightly, responding to his. He pulled back, looking into her topaz-sometimes-green eyes. Nick searched them for the truth. Not finding what he was looking for, he leaned in for another kiss when a rap on the window caused them to pull apart.

"What the heck?" Nick asked, his heart seeming to have jumped into his throat.

The concerned face of a security guard showed in the small defrosted circle on the window. "Are you all right?" he mouthed. Cat reached over and rolled down the window a bit.

"We're fine, just waiting out the storm."

"Forecast says we're in for more stormy weather. You'll never get that car out of the lot at this rate. Why don't you come inside to wait until this clears?"

"No, we'll stay here."

"Suit yourself. We have hot coffee and tea."

They heard the plows laboring to clear the lot so the cars could exit.

"We'll be fine," Cat said. Nick leaned back so the guard couldn't see his face.

The guard frowned at their short sleeves. "Don't you have a coat or anything?"

"We do, thank you," Cat said and rolled up the window.

They stayed in the car and periodically watched the plows' progress. Closer. Soon they'd be able to leave.

Just then, they heard a siren coming from inside the hospital.

"What do you suppose that's for?" Nick asked, hoping his escape hadn't been discovered yet.

After a couple of minutes, they saw the security guard and others running toward them, pointing toward the car.

"I think it's time to leave," Cat said, climbing into the front seat and putting the car in reverse. The wheels spun until she got traction from the snow. The car fishtailed as they raced toward the exit.

"What should we do?" Nick asked. He was probably in deep trouble.

The wheels slid on the ice and snow. Nick grasped the back of the seat as they spun in a semi-circle. Were they going to crash? Then the wheels found traction again. Nick could hear the wheels' vroom and engine roaring over the heater blasting hot air at them.

"You can come to my house, or I can take you home." Cat seemed to throw her words into the backseat.

"Take me home," he said. Though he couldn't imagine his parents would be pleased with his escape.

Chapter 63

Nick and Cat ran from the car to the front porch. When Nick opened the door, snow blew in with them. Once inside, they stamped and blew on their hands. There was a fire in the fireplace. Both Nick and Cat stood shivering, waving their hands at the warmth.

"Nick? What's going on?" his mom asked, coming out of the office.

"I left the hospital."

"You weren't discharged. They just called." His dad banged through the kitchen door. "Why would you do such a thing?"

"I was sick and tired of that place. The food sucks, and I just wanted to go home."

His father frowned at Cat. "That wasn't very smart of you to help him leave."

Cat suddenly seemed interested in the carpeting. "I know. I just wanted to be with him."

His father cleared his throat. "I'll call the hospital and let them know you're safe. I think you better go, Cat. We need time to digest this as a family."

She nodded, squeezed Nick's arm, and left. Nick watched as her car backed down the drive and onto the snow-covered road.

His parents sat on the couch and pointed to the chair.

"Where did you get those scrubs?" his mom asked.

"Cat."

"Hmm."

"I still don't understand," his mom said.

"Maybe you shouldn't hang around with her. She's not a very good influence," his dad added.

Nick jerked his head up. "I asked her to."

"Nick!" His mother shook her head sadly. "If you would have asked us, we would have had you discharged. There's a right and a wrong way to go about these things."

"I told you I wanted to go home!"

"What about all the strange things you were saying?" his mother asked, sad and teary-eyed. "We wanted help for that."

"You'd be confused too if you were pumped full of those drugs," Nick said, massaging his temples, feeling a headache starting in the back of his head.

His father took out his phone and called the hospital. "Hello, this is Nick Dupont's father. He arrived home safe and sound." Nick watched his father on the phone. "Yes, we're sorry for all the problems it caused the hospital. No, we'll keep him home with us. Thank you."

"Now what?" Nick asked, leaning closer to the fire and stretching out his arms.

"We'll get you an appointment with Dr. Patar, and you can discuss your feelings with her."

"What about Cat?"

"We think she may be a bad influence on you." His mother folded her arms. "What do you think?"

Nick hunched his shoulders. "Maybe."

"Nick…" his mother said. "We just want our Nick back."

"I know, me too." Nick settled back, tired of talking, yawning, and longing for his bed with soft, cushy pillows and a comforter that smelled faintly of fabric softener, not bleach and disinfectant.

Chapter 64

Here he was again—sitting in another doctor's office. This time Nick had to see Dr. Patar. The doctor routine was getting old. Instead of meeting her eyes, Nick studied the pictures of flowers on the wall.

"Hello, Nick," Dr. Patar said tentatively. "Am I talking to Nick?"

"You're talking to Nick." He did a mental shove against Jonathan.

She leaned forward as if getting a better look. "What happened at the hospital?"

"I left with Cat."

She gave him a stern look of "are you kidding me?"

"I know, I screwed up." Nick raised his hands defensively. "Cat's not good for me." Then why did he desire her again? His feelings for her were a teeter-totter. He felt unbalanced and ready to fall off at any moment.

Dr. Patar's eyes seemed to bore through his soul, and she blew out her breath. "I should be seeing Cat too!"

Could Cat come? Would Cat come?

She cleared her throat and peered down at her notes. "We tried a serotonin drug while you were in the hospital, and you responded well to it."

He remembered waking up and feeling more like

himself. Had the drug done that?

"I'd like you to continue taking serotonin." She pulled out a prescription pad, wrote something, and handed it to him.

When they finished the therapy session, he stood, thanked Dr. Patar, and pulled out his phone to call Emily when he was in the hallway.

"Hey!" he said when she answered.

Silence and then, "Nick?"

"Yeah!"

"I heard," she whispered.

"About the hospital?"

"You and Cat!" Emily said Cat, with venom in her voice.

"I only let her help me so I could get out of there and see you."

"You did?"

He heard her breathing and maybe thinking over what he said.

"You know you're my girl. Did you doubt me?"

"Well, you know, Bryan…"

"Bryan wasn't at the hospital with me."

"I know. Anyway." She paused. "Cat's not at school anymore."

That was probably for the best.

"Where is she?"

"She went to the juvenile detention center, and Veronica said she would be sent away to an uncle's farm after she got out."

Nick stifled the urge to laugh, imagining Cat milking a cow.

Chapter 65

About thirty minutes after school ended, there was a knock on the door. Nick pushed himself out of the recliner.

It could only be Emily.

But when Nick peeked out the window at the battered red truck in the drive, he knew it was Gary.

"Hey, man! How'd you know I got home?"

"Are you kidding! You know the rumor mill!" Gary brushed off the snow from his arms and wiped his boots on the mat.

"Gary!" Nick's mother said. "How have you been?"

Nick tapped his foot, waiting patiently for his mom to stop talking. When she finally left, Nick motioned for Gary to follow him up the stairs.

"What's up?"

Gary took the desk chair, and Nick sat on his bed, leaning back against the pillows. "Cat got locked up for a couple of days."

Nick raised his brows, remaining quiet, digesting the information.

"Yeah, a couple of days at juvie." Gary leaned forward. "Did she help you break out of the hospital?"

"She did."

"James Bond Dupont!" Gary slapped his knee and whistled.

"Not exactly." *It had been pretty daring. And stupid.*

Gary's brows furrowed. "Sounds like jail or something."

"I guess I was talking about all kinds of weird shit." Nick made a face.

"When can you return to school?" Gary asked.

Nick moved his shoulders around. "Soon, I hope!"

****

His grandmother came to dinner that night. "I heard you and Cat were like Bonnie and Clyde, breaking out of the hospital."

"Mother!" Nick's mom admonished.

"You were the talk of the Bunco group last night!" Grandma continued, obviously enjoying his exploits.

Nick opened his mouth to say something, but his grandmother continued, "Estelle Forest said you tied up an orderly in the bed."

"No…that's…"

"No?" Grandma looked disappointed.

"No!" Nick's mother said. "That's not what happened."

Nick made a half-hearted, strangled chuckle. His mother gave him a look, and he instantly sobered. There was no more talk of his hospital break-out that night.

Chapter 66

After bugging his parents about returning to school, they relented. He had a note from his parents explaining his absences. Nick hadn't read the message, but he could imagine what it would say: *Please excuse Nick because he thought he was Jonathan and broke out of the hospital brandishing a gun and shooting his way to freedom! Love, Grace Dupont—Nick's poor mother!*

He presented the note in the office, and the secretary said, "I hope you're feeling better, Nick."

"I am."

He left the office and was barraged by students in the hallway.

"Nick!"

"We heard!"

Coach Sullivan was standing by his classroom door when Nick walked past on his way to his locker. "Nick! Good to have you back."

Nick smiled at Coach and dipped his chin in acknowledgment.

"See you in class," Coach called. "Don't forget about football conditioning!"

Nick waved behind him and continued down the hallway to the admiring comments of his fellow students.

Emily was standing by his locker, tapping her

rainbow-hued sneakers, her arms folded, and she gave him a huge smile.

Nick leaned over, kissed her, and whispered, "I missed you."

"Me too." She returned his kiss.

They continued until someone cleared their throat. A teacher passing by gave them a stern look.

"You busted out of the hospital to be with me?" she said, looking up at him over her glasses that had slipped down her nose.

"Yup! You're my girl."

"I hope she's gone for good!" Emily said as he worked his combination lock to stow his things.

He didn't need to ask who she was referring to. "We can hope."

But the twinge in his gut told him he didn't believe she was gone for good.

"I wish she'd stay in Oregon forever," Emily said.

That would be for the best.

Nick bent down and nuzzled her cheek. "I don't want to talk about her."

She gave him a warm smile and took his hand. "What do you want to talk about?"

Anything but Cat. "How about the fun we'll have this summer?" he asked.

"We've got to make it good before our senior year!" Emily exclaimed.

"It has to be better than our junior year!" Nick said with a rueful laugh.

He rubbed his neck and moved his tense shoulders around. And said a silent prayer that Cat wouldn't spoil their senior year too.

A word about the author...

Sue writes 5-star LitPick novels that keep readers of all ages turning pages long into the night. When she's not writing, she's reading, attending author events, or walking her dogs. Snack wise, Sue is a salty-type gal, but wouldn't say no to a chocolate kiss or two! She's not sure she's a reincarnated former novelist, but if she was, she'd want to be Jane Austen, Mary Shelley, or Emily Bronte.

www.scduganauthor.wixsite.com/mysite

Thank you for purchasing
this publication of The Wild Rose Press, Inc.

For questions or more information
contact us at
info@thewildrosepress.com.

The Wild Rose Press, Inc.
www.thewildrosepress.com